Missing in Maplewood, A Novel

Maplewood Sisters, Volume 3

Elizabeth Bromke

Published by Elizabeth Bromke, 2019.

This book is a work of fiction. Names, characters, places, and events are products of the author's imagination. Any resemblance to locations, events, or people (living or dead) is purely coincidental or fictitious. Any trademarks, service marks, product names, or named features are assumed to be the property of their respective owners and are used for reference only. No implied endorsement thereof exists.

MISSING IN MAPLEWOOD

Copyright © 2019 ELIZABETH BROMKE

All rights reserved.

Cover design by GermanCreative

Cover photography by photoweges, sanneberg, and Andrew Lozovyi

The reproduction or distribution of this book without permission is a theft. If you would like to share this book or any part thereof, please contact us through our website: www.elizabethbromke.com[1]

First Edition: 2019

Published by: Elizabeth Bromke

---

1. http://www.elizabethbromke.com

For my dad, who raised me to be a tough girl.

Prologue

Everyone agreed: Erica and Ben were soul mates. But she didn't care about everyone else. She only cared about him.

Erica knew this would be the best day of her life, no matter what happened. Christmases. Promotions for Ben. Lavish vacations. With the potential exception of the births of their future children, nothing could top this day.

To both Ben and Erica, marriage was welcome and sacred. A decision never to be doubted.

There they were, at the altar, her small hands wrapped in his grip. The priest was about to announce the kiss which had Erica holding her breath. Ben hated to show affection. He didn't even hold her hand, normally. And his "I love yous" only ever came in private. This whole event was one big breath-hold for her. Did he love her enough to kiss her in front of their parents? More to the point, did he love her enough to commit here and now, before God and their witnesses, that he would always be hers? For better or worse? For richer or poorer?

In sickness and in health 'til death do they part?

Relief soon filled her. Ben didn't wait for the priest to finish directions before ducking his head down to meet her lips. He kissed her with sweet passion, their mouths parting in a brief rhythm of love. A promise. She'd have been embarrassed if it weren't so perfect. Erica was lost in his soft mouth and strong embrace.

As they pulled back from the moment to wild applause from a modest audience, he returned his head to hers, whispering, "I love you, Erica Stevens." She smiled, biting her lower lip in youthful glee. But he wasn't done, and he held her head in place next to his. "Erica, I will always take care of you, no matter what."

They floated down the aisle and out into an idling limousine then cruised over to the museum where an elegant-but-simple reception awaited the wedding party. Clean and tasteful with few decorations. Subtle lights glowed down on the dance floor, white-draped tables framed it like bubbles. Flowers filled the space, fragrance of love wafting through the air.

It was the most beautiful day of her life.

Ben had graduated the summer before. They'd planned the wedding in meticulous detail. Fall in Philadelphia. Close friends and family only. While chic and stunning was their venue and pricey was their planner, Erica maintained that the day be about their love, nothing more, nothing less.

Everything came together gloriously, but, in fact, Erica hadn't much cared about the wedding, after all. Now, as she danced with her new husband, the only thing she could think about was the life they'd build together. She was so happy to marry Ben Stevens, and he was so happy to marry her.

They loved each other.

Chapter 1: Erica

"Clinically, it sounds like postpartum depression. Practically, I'd suggest you think hard about your marriage."

Inauthentic southwestern décor splashed across the tacky medical suite, momentarily distracting Erica Stevens. But now her focus narrowed on the psychobabblist.

"Do you mean *leave him*?" Surely a medical professional, psychologist or otherwise, wouldn't presume to take on the role of marital counselor. Yet, something about the suggestion sank in.

"Erica, you're smart and independent. You need to think about yourself in order to stand a chance at happiness. Besides, you're in a new town. You have the chance to start fresh."

Erica stood, indicating to the silver-haired therapist that the session was over. She'd like her pill prescription and to move on with her day, thankyouverymuch. Pinot noir was chilling in the fridge. A backlog of DVR recordings simmered on her TV at home. The kids were at day camp until five.

Sweeping her white-blonde, A-line cut back off her neck, she made her way to the black Escalade that Ben had bought her as a moving gift. She loved it. She loved him, too. She really did.

But she didn't want to move back to Arizona, much less *Tucson*, Arizona, with its west coast vibe and smothering summer heat. Over the past ten years, Philadelphia had become her home. He tried to convince her that she'd appreciate being closer to her family, who lived a four-hour drive north, in Maplewood. She had fought him with all her might. Her friends were in Philly. She needed to be in a big city, not a maze of suburbs. Besides, maybe she'd finally enroll in a few teaching courses come fall. Finally work toward her teacher certification after putting it off for over ten years.

But, it wasn't a choice. He got the promotion—from assistant to head coach. *In their home state, Erica!* He'd urged her. Arizona just didn't feel like her home any more.

It was a more-than-disappointing return. Erica missed their two-story brownstone walk-up. She missed being a stroll away from fine dining and art shows and the theatre. She missed everything that she had missed because she grew up in a mountain town. Philly was a far cry from weekend camping trips and small-town gossip. And though she missed the camping, she didn't miss the gossip.

Of course, Erica could just as easily enroll in classes at Southwestern. And Tucson had theatre and fine dining. But change was hard on Erica, especially after losing the baby. Every little thing felt like a really big thing. And moving was already a really big thing. Once again, Erica was following Ben. Her hopes and dreams didn't matter.

As she pulled out of the plaza and onto Oracle Road, a call chirped through her Bluetooth. It was Bo.

She clicked her sister on the line, glad for the one thing Tucson had to offer: her best friend. "Hey, what's up?"

"Are you done with the shrink?"

"She's a therapist, Roberta. Have some tact." Erica teased, silently agreeing that it was absolutely ridiculous she had to talk to a mental health professional. She was fine. Really, she was.

Bo laughed at her own lame joke. "Whatever. Let's do lunch. I can come to you. I've got a break in my schedule."

Bo lived right next to Southwestern University and claimed to be a writer for the Sonoran Sun-Times, although she rarely seemed to work.

Erica flinched as a low-flying bird nearly smacked into her side-view mirror. *Jeez*. Nature had been less a part of the last decade of her life. Living in the center of Philly had only acquainted her with pigeons, who scavenged more than they flew.

She shook her head and returned her attention to Bo. "Sure, but give me a few minutes to get home and set up. I don't have much in the fridge. How does wine and Red Vines sound?" Her sister agreed with enthusiasm and replied she'd be up soon.

Absently, Erica navigated through the mess of lunchtime traffic, northward, out of the city limits and back into her new suburb, Golden Valley: Tucson's answer to Scottsdale. She had to admit Golden Valley was quickly growing on her. It was super posh, but it also felt *safe*: two things that almost made up for what she had lost.

Half an hour later, Erica stretched her limber body out on a chaise lounge that didn't go with the adobe hacienda. Of course, none of Erica's custom-designed *east coast* furniture fit in with the pottery-laden, ranch-style casas of southern Arizona.

Bo, who'd walked in moments earlier, grabbed a bouquet of Red Vines and plucked her wine glass from the counter before plopping onto the adjacent sofa.

The older Delaney sister gnawed on a strand of licorice and replied to Erica's bombshell therapist advice. "She said *what*?"

"She thought I should leave him. That we're past the point of no return," Erica answered blankly, striving for nonchalance, as she clicked through her DVR library until she found *The Real Housewives* episode she had missed during the move.

Don't cry. Don't cry. Don't cry.

"And did you *ask* her for advice on the matter? I thought you were just going to get a refill of Xanax."

"I mean it came up again. This was the second time I've met with her, and it came up. I needed a third-party sounding board." Exasperated now, Erica examined her manicure, regretting her transition from French tips to deep red. She felt like a tart, as her mother would say. Of course, she regretted a lot more than the manicure. Quite a lot.

"Erica, *I* am your third-party sounding board. And I think your psycho doctor overstepped her boundaries, and I think you would be insane to divorce Ben. How can you be frustrated with him? He's never around. You need to get a grip." Bo leaned back into the sofa, satisfied, as though she had solved the matter.

But what she couldn't solve was Erica's heartache. Only Ben could do that, and he had hardly tried. Resentment swelled in her slight chest as she prepared to battle her sister on this point.

"That's the problem, Bo. He's never around. He never talks. We never see each other. After losing the baby, Ben's answer was to travel across the country to chase a new position. In a different state. Away from the home we made. The home where we would have had our little girl." Erica's voice cracked, but she swallowed hard, navigating her remote to the TV.

Bo pushed off the sofa, joining Erica on the chaise. She wrapped her arm around her younger sister, a fresh Red Vine dangling over Erica's shoulder. Erica's crystal blue eyes stared toward the TV, unseeing. Her voice soft, Bo whispered, "Erica, you don't know if it was a girl or a boy."

Erica dropped the remote, leaning away and twisting to meet Bo's gaze. "Screw you." Her voice quaked, and Erica forced herself to slow down and talk it out. *Breathe.* "I'm sorry, Bo. It's just that..." She glanced around the sterile house before letting her gaze fall into her lap. "It's just that *we were* happy. Everything would have been fine. All I needed was a little attention in the wake of the most awful thing I had ever been through. And maybe a little support for *my* dreams, for once." Erica's face flushed, and she pushed off her cushioned seat, striding to the wet bar to refill her empty glass.

Erica Stevens was not a crier. Never had been. Hadn't even cried much after losing her baby at a delicate ten weeks, two weeks shy of the announcement party she'd planned. One week shy of Ben admitting he'd been contacted by the Arizona football program.

A realization poked up from the pit of her stomach. *Maybe she should have cried then.* She pushed it back down.

Speaking without turning around, Erica finalized her stance. "Bo, you don't understand. Fixing things with Ben isn't possible. Not after the miscarriage. Not after the move." As the words fell from her mouth, it occurred to her that she sounded like she was holding a grudge. Like she was petty. Like it was this one thing in an otherwise perfect life that would push her to divorce.

But what Erica wasn't saying was all the little stuff. All the little cracks that erupt within a marriage, not a single one to blame for the inevitable, massive earthquake. No, Bo could never understand that. She hadn't had so much as a long-term relationship, much less a marriage. She had no idea.

Sipping calmly at the bar, Erica heard Bo move behind her, grabbing her keys from the side table and opening the door. "If you want to throw away your life, I'm not sticking around to watch."

Erica turned to stop her, her mouth falling open. Her face wrinkled in disgust at Bo's refusal to take her side. As she stalled in the open doorway, a warm June breeze blew the Bo's jet black locks across her face.

"Erica, Ben's a good guy. Don't listen to that therapist." She slammed the door, leaving Erica to crumple onto the Saltillo tile, sobs finally wracking her lithe body.

Chapter 2: Ben

Ben Stevens folded his long, tired body into the Bobcat-red BMW sedan. Southwestern University had thrown it in with his sign-on bonus, and he still felt obligated to drive it to and from work each day. The disparity did not escape him. Erica would fit better in the Beemer, and he'd fit better in the massive Caddy. Sadly, it wasn't the only disparity in their marriage.

He sped along the dimly lit grid that made up Tucson's road system, sliding his phone into the cup holder next to him before noticing the missed call and message notification. His eyes trained ahead, he blindly opened the voicemail and pressed play.

Hey Benji, I know you're coaching. Just calling to say hi. Hope all is well. How those boys doin'? I mean your sons, not your team. Call me back when you can.

Ben smiled. His dad left a near-identical voicemail every night. Ben was generally good about getting back in touch. He'd always return his dad's call the very next day. Sometimes when he was on the field during water breaks. Sometimes in the locker room before or after practice.

Twenty minutes and two key-coded entry gates later, the Stevens four-car garage sucked him into its empty darkness. Ben tried to creep undetected through the hall and to his own sleeping quarters, separate from Erica's. God forbid he woke her. It would mean another stupid fight, no doubt.

Despite Erica's protests to the contrary, little had changed from their life in Philly. They were still not sleeping together (a mutual decision, to be fair). They were still not seeing each other (okay, his fault). And they were still arguing any time they happened to cross paths. Other than the scenery, life was no different. What was she complaining about? Irritation curled his lips before he even reached his room.

THREE HOURS AFTER COLLAPSING on top of the designer duvet, his phone alarm stunned him awake. Groggily, Ben showered, shaved, and dressed before shuffling to the kitchen where he planned to rush through a protein bar and black coffee before flying back down to the U. He could see why many coaches slept at the office. This was brutal. But, he had to admit, he loved it. He loved coaching. He loved the long hours. He loved working the greatest sport on earth. It was quite possibly the best part of his life. Other than the twins, of course.

But once he passed from the hallway and landed at the edge of the kitchen counter, he jolted for the second time in twenty minutes. There at the breakfast bar was Erica, perched like a tired, blonde bird, her arms hugged closely around her torso. *Here we go*, he murmured to himself before forcing a weak smile.

"Hey. What're you doing up?" Cautiously, Ben carried on in his routine, swallowing the uneasy feeling that grew in his gut and climbed up to his throat. Couldn't Erica just live her life, already? Go shopping. Get her nails done. Cart the boys down to the Reid Park Zoo or the local splash park or whatever the hell it was called? Minding each other's own business had become far more comfortable. Right?

And then she hit him with it. The dreaded four words no man ever wanted to hear, and especially before the start of another grueling day at work, even if it was a job he loved.

"We need to talk."

He focused his eyes on the coffee maker, moving purposefully to it. Usually, this type of attack would come out of the blue on the weekend or if they happened to see each other after work in the middle of the week. Never in the early morning. Still, with each nag, he felt transported to the movie *Groundhog Day*. Before the baby, she'd whine about generally stupid things. Things out of his control. Their script was written. The actors cast.

Erica: **Couldn't he get home earlier?**
Ben: **No, he couldn't.**
Erica: **Why not take a day off?**
Ben: **Obviously that was a ridiculous suggestion.**
Erica: **Tell them you're sick.**
Ben (an aside): *The only thing I'm sick of is you.* [Cue audience laughter.]

Then, once she was pregnant, the shtick updated slightly. It turned into a poorly thought-out sequel, revolving around his apathy toward the new baby. Didn't he want a daughter, too? As badly as she did?

Honestly, he didn't care. Well, sure, he *wanted* the baby. But he had a lot on his plate as it was.

Then, after the baby, a darker and more dramatic shift. Act III. The final chapter, really. They argued about her grief and how long she was "allowed" to mourn. About how he *didn't* grieve. About how he didn't want to talk about it. About what was going to happen next?

He'd convinced himself that the move would fix it all. Give them the change their marriage so desperately needed.

Of course, that wasn't the real reason Ben secretly reached out to Southwestern in the middle of last season. He wanted a promotion. He wanted to be the boss- no more taking orders from an old man who hadn't kept up with the demands of coaching football in the modern era. Ben was ready to take over. The fact that he'd caught wind of Southwestern losing their head coach seemed like destiny. To be a head football coach, even at a college, in his thirties in his home state? He was beside himself with glee. He had tried to leverage the fact that the offer came from a city near their home town.

It hadn't worked. Erica didn't want to go back to Arizona. This didn't surprise him. He was well aware how much she loved Philly. Sadly for her, he didn't care. This was the plan. If Erica wanted it another way, then she could stay behind.

"Okay," he started, ready for World War III. He felt her brush up behind him as she pulled a stout white mug from the cabinet above the coffee pot.

He opened to her, watching as her smooth hand reached out, its red-tipped fingers resting briefly on his forearm. Electricity coursed through his veins. Was this a ploy? He had to admit, no matter how bad things were in their marriage, Ben had always been *attracted* to her. Ever since they were kids, Ben wanted Erica for his own. And it wasn't just her beauty, either. There was a softness to Erica, in her touch, even when she was complaining, that used to melt him. *Used to.*

He shook the feeling, geared up for battle, and tried to head her off at the pass, knowing full well that distraction could be incredibly powerful- in football games, in war, and in marriage. "Did you get your prescription refilled, babe? How'd you sleep last night?"

"Yes, I got my pills. But, I did not sleep well. Ben," she dropped her hand, wrapping her long, slim fingers around her mug and holding the empty vessel against her t-shirt. He couldn't help but notice she was braless beneath. He flashed his eyes back to hers. "Ben, I can't move on, and it's time we talk about it."

He played dumb, following their script.

"Talk about what?" The coffee had finally started to drip into the carafe, its stuttering rhythm cutting through the tension or adding to it. He didn't know which. His heart raced. He was so *sick* of talking about the baby.

"You *know* what, Ben." She sighed deeply, her arched brows furrowing. Her mouth set in a thin, pink line.

Ben cleared this throat. "Erica, hon," he started, gentle as ever. "What did the doctor say? Is there another medication that might help? Maybe you should spend more time with the boys, or..."

She sliced her hand up through the air, her palm facing him. His mind briefly jumped to an errand he had to run that morning, wondering if he should cancel it or be late for work. Resentment clouded his mind, and he considered cancelling.

"Don't patronize me, Ben."

With that, something flipped. He went off script.

"Erica, enough of this crap. You lost a baby. *We* lost a baby. It sucked. I know. I was there. And I even got you..." he paused momentarily, changing course. "And instead of welcoming a fresh start in your *home* state, you drag out your misery and allow it to consume you, me, and the two children who ARE alive."

He monitored her face, waiting for an explosion of female proportions.

But, she held it together. Somewhat. Besides a deep breath and a flare of her nostrils, she kept her cool.

"Newsflash, Ben... I *was* happy. Happy to grieve in *our home* in Pennsylvania. Happy to finally start looking into my own career. Happy to have a healthy distance from our backwoods upbringing, and happy to let my friends nurse me back to health, since I knew quite well that my own husband didn't give two rat turds."

He stifled a snicker, in spite of himself. No matter how angry Erica was, her sense of humor prevailed. Back in high school, it was one of the characteristics that turned him from infatuated to all-out smitten. It was part of the reason he married her. Erica could always make him laugh.

But she wasn't trying to be funny right now, and he wouldn't have laughed if she was cracking a joke. This was dire.

"I gave it everything, Erica, and you know it. I accepted the job offer *to help us*. We needed something new. Losing the baby was awful. No doubt. But, we were already living separate lives in Philly." That would get her to see. The promotion was a good thing. It wasn't just about money or fame or control. It was about starting over, too. That was true even if it wasn't the main reason he'd taken the SU job. They could take the move as a chance to reconnect. She could easily start her coursework in Arizona.

But, no. It didn't work. They were more miserable than ever. He braced himself for whatever was next by pouring a cup of coffee and taking a slow sip, his gaze on the counter.

Erica set her mug down. She was calm. Scary calm.

"We are living separate lives *here*," she growled, crossing her arms and leaning toward him. "You have moved on to bigger and better things. Which was easy for you, because you didn't care about having more kids. Ben, I think you were even *happy* about my miscarriage."

Ben froze. His blood turning to ice. He couldn't let her get away with that.

It fell out of his mouth before he could contain it. "I think *you* were the happy one."

The idea wasn't so far-fetched. Erica seemed to love the attention, after all. And she kept talking about chasing her own dreams- teaching, especially. Yet, he knew he'd overstepped. Out of anger and self-defense. It wasn't true. Erica had been devastated. Tears or no tears, they had lost a little life. Sure, Erica got mileage out of it, but at the ultimate cost. The weeks and months after losing the baby were very bad. A loving marriage felt a million miles away. He had no idea how to help her, but, if he was honest, he was losing interest. Even so, it wasn't fair to be cruel.

He rubbed his hands up across his face, ready to apologize. Kiss and make up. Move on. Deal with it later.

But she didn't give him a chance.

Erica Stevens locked eyes with her husband. "I want a divorce."

Chapter 3: Erica

"I can't believe it." Bo blew out a breath from the front seat of the Escalade. "I'm so sad for you. Both of you."

A deep frown set across Erica's mouth. "You barely knew him, Bo. We've lived our entire marriage away from you and everyone else. No one knows how bad it was. How hateful he can be."

She had called her older sister as soon as Ben trudged off to work. They were both defeated. After she had said those four damning words, she couldn't well take them back, even if part of her wanted to. And, a big part of her *did* want to take them back. She knew Ben was not evil. He was probably speaking out of anger. But words hurt. Erica had cried again, slow, weepy tears, as she texted Bo that "it" happened.

Her older sister drove straight up to Golden Valley, joining Erica as she trucked Nicky and Luke to day camp at the Methodist church. While the boys were with them, she kept her mouth shut. No sense in worrying them. Erica had considered keeping them home with her. She needed someone to cuddle with. But they loved their little camp. She couldn't break Nicky's and Luke's hearts just because hers was broken.

Now Erica and Bo sat alone on the leather seats in the air-conditioned cabin, aimlessly steering around town. Bo should have been at her own place, working on her current piece for the Sonoran Sun-Times. But there she was with Erica. Offering no sympathy. Judging, instead.

"Barely knew him? We literally grew up together. Do you have a concussion? Because that would explain why you would go to such extremes."

Erica huffed, delicately pushing the pad of her pinky under her eyes to prevent them from welling up yet again. She had pulled it together, put on her war paint and set about moving forward, however she could. "Extremes? This was cemented months ago when I first got pregnant and Ben acted like it was an inconvenience. Maybe even a year ago when he brushed off my idea of going back to school for my degree." Her mouth fell into a pout. Her mind flashed back. He'd told her there was no point in her working. He made good money. She ought to be happy as she was. "I don't want to talk about it. What's done is done. I need a lawyer. Google the Arizona Bar Association for me."

Bo didn't move to pull her phone from her satchel.

"Fine, I will." Erica stabbed a button her steering wheel. "Siri," she started, waiting for her device to wake up.

"How can I help you, ERICA?"

Bo made a face. "Creepy." Erica shushed her.

"Google TUCSON DIVORCE ATTORNEY."

"I'm sorry to hear that," the computer chirped back robotically.

Erica slammed her hands on the wheel, but didn't answer, waiting for the search engine to offer a savior.

"Here are over 100 results matching your search. Would you like me to dial the nearest TUCSON DIVORCE ATTORNEY?" Siri's voice shifted into full-on terminator-mode with the last three words.

Erica swerved the SUV into the shopping plaza they were about to pass, her mouth quivering, goosebumps peppering her flesh. The Starbucks logo shone like a beacon, welcoming her into its familiar comfort. But nothing was comfortable right now. She pushed the shaft into park and swooped up the phone from its cradle on the console.

Not yet, she thought to herself as she carefully rifled through the search results. Bo opened the door and stalked over the steaming asphalt and into the coffee shop.

Erica glanced through the names that her phone had returned for her, looking for a sign. An omen. Anything to shake her out of the misery or commit her to it further.

Brad Herrera, 2 stars
Yeah right.
Donald Harvey, 4 stars
Soft maybe.
Reba McGrath, 5 stars
Hard Maybe.

Just as Erica hovered the pad of her finger over the power button to screenshot Reba McGraths's contact information, a text flashed across her screen.

Ben: **Call me. 911.**

Erica's heart stopped, and she sucked in a breath, her chest rising and falling.

The boys? It couldn't be. She *just* dropped them off, and *she* was the emergency contact at the church.

Her parents? No. Why would Ben find out about anything before she did?

His job? A silent prayer escaped her lips. That would solve everything. If he quit coaching. Retired. Gave his full attention to his family. To her.

Maybe this emergency text would save them.

She swiped out of the search results and clicked on the text before tapping Ben's name.

The line didn't even ring. Ben's voice came on immediately, cracking as he launched into the news.

His father was rushed to the ER. A pulmonary embolism. He was in the ICU at Maplewood Regional. It didn't look good. The priest was en route to give last rites. Family was gathering at the hospital.

Erica's heart sank deeper into her chest. Despite it all, she loved Ben's family nearly as much as her own. This was bad. Very bad.

Nearly speechless, she let the line go silent for a beat and adjusted the phone along her jaw, measuring what to say next.

A thought occurred to her. Ben had a private pilot's license. He could easily charter a plane and get to Maplewood within the span of two hours. He could go now. Quickly. Alone. She'd stay with the boys. He could handle it. Jumping ahead, she saw herself driving the twins up to Maplewood for a funeral in the coming days. But something flipped inside her. A proactive measure, of sorts. Hope, even.

"I'll go with you," she said, at last. The boys could stay with Bo. She'd leave here and now. She'd step out of herself for the moment and help her husband. But her offer was met only with silence from the other end. Was he crying?

She heard shuffling over the line, Ben's voice to a woman, thanking her, before he came back on.

"Who was that?" Erica asked. She'd assumed he was already in his office, planning out practice for the day.

"Just had to pick something up from the post office," Ben cleared his throat. He sniffed before continuing, "Erica, you don't have to, especially since..." his voice trailed off, shattering something fragile between them.

Just then, Bo poked her head out of the Starbucks, waving frantically at Erica as she jogged up to the car.

"Just a second, Ben," she held the phone away as Bo pulled up to a stop at her opening window.

Breathless, the older sister choked out, "I just saw a Facebook post. Ben's dad's at the hospital. It's serious."

Erica glared meaningfully at Bo before gesturing to her phone. "I'm on the phone with him. We're figuring out what to do." In a flash, Bo reached through the window and grabbed the little black device.

"Ben, this is Bo. Do you still have your pilot's license?" A pause allowed Erica to lift her eyebrows in surprise at her sister's sharp memory. Bo pressed on. "Good. Erica can meet you at the La Cienega Regional Airpark in ten minutes. I have a connection there." She clicked END before waiting for a response from either Ben or Erica and jogged around the car, hopping into the front seat and directing Erica to hang a left out of the plaza, a right on Calle de la Hacienda and another left onto Canyon del Oro.

Shock took over, and Erica didn't argue. Although, she was impressed with Bo's quick thinking. Maybe Bo did know him a little better than she'd thought. Maybe, too, she was turning her life around. Being a helper rather than a continual victim of her circumstances. As if reading Erica's mind, her sister chimed in, assuring her she'd pick up the boys, take them home and keep them safe. Not to worry. Erica thanked her, breathless with anxiety.

Once they pulled down the dirt road and toward a massive hangar, something occurred to her. She frowned and looked over to her older sister.

"Who do you know that has something to do with a private airpark? Or airplane?"

Bo sucked in a deep breath before delivering a measured reply. "I'm taking a course at Tucson Community College. My instructor lives here. He has a little plane. We meet to workshop my writing at his in-home office. Don't worry about it."

Erica was too distracted to question her. Ben had pulled up behind them, dust billowing beneath his low profile BMW. He must have sped like a bat out of hell. The drive from the university all the way up to La Cienega was at least thirty minutes, if you followed the speed limit.

A shiver coursed through her body.

Chapter 4: Ben

His dad couldn't die. No way. Ben hadn't even seen him in well over a year. Maybe two. Come to think of it, he couldn't remember when he last visited Maplewood. Once they'd moved to Tucson, his parents and Erica's harped on them to drive or fly up for a day visit. They wanted to see the boys.

But the new job was too crazy. Preseason was well underway. He couldn't leave town. He'd asked his family to drive south to Tucson, but the Stevenses were notorious homebodies. Sadly. The plan was always "Maybe soon." Or "Yeah, that'd be nice." Neither party ever made solid plans to visit the other. Shame now coated Ben's heart.

As his GPS instructed him to turn down a dusty lane, his face hardened. He didn't want Erica to go with him. He was disgusted with her. Half a year of bitchy behavior and nagging and drinking wine and watching reality shows. He was the one who deserved to be fed up. And he was.

But Bo had taken over on handling the situation, and he had no choice. Anyway, he needed someone to call the shots now. Someone to take control and get him to Maplewood. That was all that mattered.

Even after moving across the country, Ben was as close to his father as a man could be. His dad had taught him to play the sport he loved, setting him up for a college scholarship and a successful career, and how had he thanked him? By returning daily phone calls? That was it? Ben could do better. He should have visited Maplewood sooner. He should have insisted that Dad join him in Tucson. He also knew he should be building a relationship between his sons and his father. But he'd let family fall to the backseat. He swallowed hard.

On the way from the post office, he'd called his associate head coach to let him know. Now Ben needed to focus on getting to the mountain. Getting to his dad. Making it there in time. It wouldn't hurt to have a copilot, anyway. He hadn't flown in several months, after all. Erica would have an opportunity to prove her worth a little, not that it would change anything.

Ben twisted his hands on the leather steering wheel, training his eyes on the hangar ahead of the Caddy. It was small, and the area was desolate. Nothing like the park he'd trained at or the private one where he'd kept his plane outside Philly. He'd sold it before the move. He just didn't have time to fly anymore. Now, he wished he'd brought it. The ones that lined the hangar didn't hold a candle to his baby.

After pulling into a dirt lot near the entry, Ben hopped out, grabbed his coaching duffle bag—which held not only the package from the post office but also his wallet, cell, charger, and a couple bottles of Gatorade—and dashed up to the passenger side of the SUV, opening the door for Bo as she fell out.

"I talked to Harry and you can borrow his Piper Cherokee if you have the right license. I have no idea what that means." Bo and Ben walked and talked together, her eyes and his searching for whoever was around to help.

After flagging down the only person in the place, Bo talked her way through the plan, briefly putting in a call to her friend before convincing the guy to walk the two over to a shabby two-seater registered to Harrison Vogel.

Ben stole a glance over his shoulder to find Erica stalking toward him in a skimpy exercise outfit and sandals. A designer purse slapped against her tanned thigh. In other circumstances this view of her might force a truce. She managed to look hot in just a tank top and spandex, her hair loose and fluttering across her face. He bit his lip. An image of his father, unconscious and gasping for breaths, came into his mind. This was the worst day of his life.

In fewer than ten minutes, they'd bid farewell to Bo and the attendant. Bo said she'd figure out details for them and contact the church to pick up the boys.

He wasted no time stowing his duffle and her purse in the rear compartment before climbing in. He let Bo help Erica get situated before passing her the headphones.

When she grabbed them, she covered his hand with hers. "Ben, I'm so sorry," she searched for his eyes, before adding, "I promise it will be okay. He'll pull through."

"Just buckle up," he directed, all but ignoring her in order to keep his own tears at bay. He didn't have time to be weak.

After a couple shots of prime, the engine coughed to life. Ben watched the gauges flutter then stabilize as the engine settled down to a rhythmic hum. Ben turned on the navigation lights and radio as he stowed the checklist under his kneeboard.

Take-off was smooth, and he let the plane ascend before grabbing the radio.

"La Cienega area traffic: Piper Cherokee, eh," he began as he glanced down to the craft's name before continuing. "La Cienega area traffic: November 1437 Hotel is departing La Cienega Airpark northbound. Acknowledge." He waited.

Erica slowly turned to face him, expectant.

Nothing.

"What's wrong?" She broke in, speaking loudly into her headset. Feeling himself grow warm, he shushed her with a hand.

"This is Piper Cherokee November 1437 Hotel departing to the north."

More silence. The radio clicked to life. Static broke through.

The stuttering of a man's voice crackled out as quickly as it had come on.

"Who exactly does this airplane belong to?" he demanded of Erica, knowing she probably didn't have a clue. He turned his face to her, studying the blonde wisps of hair as they blew across her face, sticking to her glossy mouth. Sunlight framed her pretty face, stilling him for a brief moment.

She held her microphone nearer her mouth. "Bo's writing teacher, I guess."

Ben grunted. Bo had long since graduated from college. "What do you know about him?"

"Nothing." Erica's voice rose, though Ben couldn't tell if it was in anger or because of the engine which rumbled even louder as they pitched to crest Dove Mountain.

"Well, do you know if he is reliable? I have never flown a plane with a malfunctioning radio." Ben pulled his sunglasses from the pocket of his t-shirt as they met with a fierce, mid-morning Arizona sun peeking from atop the Catalina Mountains to the east.

"Do you really think I know? Bo has always kept her personal life personal. Total mystery. That he's a college instructor should mean something, right?"

Ben snorted. "Erica, are you that dumb?"

He peaked over at his soon-to-be-ex to catch her expression. Splotchy redness stained her bare neck as she whipped her head to him.

"What's that supposed to mean?"

"Erica, she's obviously *seeing* him." Ben let satisfaction fill his face on this one, allowing for the distraction to keep him from breaking down. Bo had never been like the Anna Delaney—a true flirt—but she was no Mary or Erica. As high school sweethearts, Erica and Ben were each other's one-and-onlys. A frown replaced his smugness, and he swallowed hard, realizing what it may mean if the divorce really happened. His stomach lurched as Erica launched into a drawn-out reply about privacy and respecting that her family was secretive in nature.

A thought occurred to him, but he tried to push it off. It would only enrage him more if it were true.

"What?" She pressed from beside him. Mind reader. His lip pricked up in a smirk. Now wasn't the time to get into it. He had other things to worry about.

"Nothing."

Erica's sigh crackled into his ear. "No, you were about to say something. What?"

Fine. He'd ask. If she wanted to make him even more upset, then she could just have right at it. "Have you told Bo that you asked me for a divorce?"

Chapter 5: Erica

Well, she gave him points for being perceptive. But it was only Bo. Not like she had shared it with her parents or anyone else.

As far as they knew, everything had settled in after the miscarriage.

If they *did* go forward with the divorce, she couldn't deal with breaking the news. It would kill her parents. Erica didn't know if it were physical distance that made her emotionally distant from her family, or if it was her pride. Either way, she didn't want anyone to cry for her or fly into ridiculous shows of pity or yell at her or whatever. She'd wanted that from *Ben*. She wanted emotion from her own husband for once. He thought moving to Arizona was all that was needed to fix their marriage. He couldn't be more wrong.

After high school, Ben had been sad to leave Maplewood, football scholarship or not. Erica couldn't relate. All she had wanted was a change of scenery. She wanted to see the world. To learn. One day, she saw herself as a teacher, maybe.

But that wasn't all. Most importantly, she wanted the love of her life by her side. It was the perfect scenario, and Erica had thrown her efforts into being part of their twosome. She'd follow Ben anywhere. And when Philadelphia called with a job offer, all of her dreams came true.

To Erica, it felt like life had finally started. She went from clipping coupons to picking out antique furniture from a private dealer in New York City. *New York City*!

Then, Ben proposed, and Erica happily planned a small, elegant wedding at the Philadelphia Museum of Art. It was the first step in her new life. She explored various museums around the city, and then became a patron of the Philadelphia Ballet and a couple smaller theatres.

In Maplewood, Erica was just the quarterback's girlfriend. In Philadelphia, she was *someone*. She volunteered at the Children's Museum, making kids laugh and smile while they learned on the amateur tours she gave.

Once she became pregnant with the twins, Ben discouraged her from going back to school to finish her degree. Instead, she'd get to be a spoiled stay-at-home mom, he'd convinced her.

She bought it. She was happy, even. Really, she was.

They built a perfect life in Philly, and her family was well aware of that.

Then the miscarriage happened. The first crack in the façade. To admit any other difficulty or bump or even tragedy was to admit total failure. So, Erica worked on dealing with it as well as she could. On her own, mostly.

She inquired about the teaching program at St. Mary's. Set a counseling appointment. Completed her registration. The twins were in a great public school where she would someday like to teach, perhaps. She could accept that Ben was moving on from the loss of his daughter, as long as she was allowed to keep her plan.

Of course, once Southwestern offered Ben the new job, her plans no longer mattered. Just as her deeply rooted grief over the baby had not mattered.

The Stevens and the Delaneys in Maplewood assumed he had arranged for the move so that they could raise the twins closer to family and so that Erica would have the support of her mother and sisters in the wake of losing the little baby.

Now, as they flew through the Arizona sky, she considered his question. She told Bo, yes. But there was no way she could tell anyone else. How could Erica break more bad news? How could she tell them that not only was she incapable of keeping a baby alive, but she was also incapable of keeping her marriage alive? It felt impossible. She bit her lip and stared out of her window, realizing that this trip would finalize everything, one way or the other.

Ben blew air from his mouth and fiddled with dials on the dashboard before pinching his microphone between his fingers.

"This is Ben Stevens, en route to Maplewood Regional, come in, over."

He was too distracted to care much more about what Bo knew, and he brushed it off easily. Ignoring her once again. This time, however, she didn't mind. Maybe she would gain the courage to tell her parents once they made it to Maplewood. Somewhere between the quiet drive to the airpark and their take-off, she figured that Ben's dad's situation would sort of help to overshadow the separation and lessen the blow and drama. At the very least, his poor health would put divorce into perspective. Couldn't be as bad as a death. Could it?

"Still nothing, wow," Ben muttered before fiddling again with the dials and buttons. Erica didn't respond, but a sinking feeling began to form a puddle in the pit of her stomach. Who *was* Bo's 'friend?'

Ben uttered a curse and flexed his hand on throttle. Erica noticed the tension in his forearms. She felt a pang of guilt.

He coughed. "You shouldn't have come."

Her eyebrows wrinkled in, and she shook her head. "What?"

"Well, if this thing goes down and we both die, then the boys will have no one. You shouldn't have come. I could have gone by myself."

"Thanks for making me feel confident in our safety," she spat, tucking her cheeks in-between her teeth and flaring her nostrils. "Is something wrong?" She searched the dash as if she could spot some technical failure.

He licked his lips. "Not yet, but I don't like that we don't have a stable radio connection. Not ideal."

Erica rolled her eyes. Whatever. She couldn't wait for the flight to be over. She was starving. She didn't normally skip breakfast, but how could she eat after declaring she wanted a divorce? She flicked a glance to her husband, wondering if he was thinking about it, too.

"Ben?"

"What, Erica?" he grunted, his eyes trained on the landscape before them.

"Do you want to talk about... you know, our conversation this morning?"

Ben flinched, and the plane dipped down and up in one jerk of his wrist. Erica felt her stomach cartwheel through her torso. A bad rollercoaster.

"See that? Don't bother me. No," he answered, sweat beading along the back of his neck.

Erica set her jaw and leaned back into her seat, deciding to watch their journey over crags and saguaros and rocky terrain. They hadn't been in the air long, and she could easily tell they hadn't come far. She could spot the casino that lay north of Tucson, Desert Rhinestone. They were flying close enough for her to identify a few cars as they crept up and down the miniature town of Mammoth, Arizona. Little bugs going about their daily business.

How she wished she were going about her daily business. If only she could go back in time a few hours, she would probably change something. Maybe she should have just moved on from her pain. Kept her mouth shut. Worked through it without Ben, like she would have done in Philly.

Maybe daily, low-grade unhappiness was better than feeling like you were about to fall off a cliff only to hit true rock bottom.

Chapter 6: Bo

Bo had placed a call to the church to see about picking up the twins at the end of the day. Erica managed to shoot a text before she left so the camp coordinator knew to expect Aunt Bo that evening. She had all day to kill and nowhere to be.

Yes, an article on Sonoran Hot Dogs was waiting to be fleshed out. How do you even write a full-length piece on the virtue of southwestern wieners? She let out a sigh.

Bo had been writing for the Sonoran Sun Times for well over a year. She covered the fluff pieces and was hanging by a thread. To cover living expenses, she had also taken up content writing for a locally based marketing firm. She was fired after breaking off a romantic fling with one of their major clients.

Now, all she had were crap assignments with a crap newspaper that would be replaced by a crap online competitor in the near future.

Oh, well. More of the same for the oldest Delaney girl. Bo didn't even mind. She liked bumping around from city to city, trying new things, as long as they weren't sloppy foot-longs with soggy jalapenos.

As soon as she'd touched base with the day camp, she drove the Caddy back to Erica's development, where she promptly forgot the entry gate code. The security officer was on break and nowhere to be seen, so Bo decided to take the SUV for a joyride and check in with the real hero of the day, Instructor Vogel.

Once she was fired from the marketing firm, she decided she had enough time and just enough cash to pay for a writing course at the community college. It wouldn't hurt to hone her craft. Maybe she'd get a lead on a new job.

The class was useless, filled to the brim with nineteen year-olds who had barely graduated from high school. However, the teacher was decidedly the hottest man she had ever met in her life. Instructor Vogel (no, he didn't have his doctorate... *yet*) had managed to revive her faith in her writing abilities and in her career selection. He poured over her flash fiction pieces and gushed about her short stories.

Basically, Bo was falling in love.

Just before the Southwestern Writing Convention's award ceremony, Harry (as he'd told Bo to call him) nominated her for Best Emerging Voice in Tucson. To win, she needed to write a short story on The Importance of Place and she needed to write it well. He offered to give her one-on-one support.

She took him up on it.

During their long hours at his office and even a few meetings in his home, the flirtation grew.

The stares she earned from her classmates condemned her squarely to SCANDAL status. This, of course, gave Bo a thrill and encouraged her to flaunt their budding relationship in small ways, like nodding her head vigorously from the first row of desks as Harry introduced his unit on romance writing.

Since the start of the semester, the prospects of a serious relationship were good. And so, when she saw the Facebook post requesting prayers for Ben's dad, she knew exactly what to do. At first, she was going to ask Harry to fly Ben and Erica to Maplewood, and then she somehow recalled that Ben had his license. Voila.

Except, when she finally reached Harry as they made their way into the hangar, he was less than thrilled to "entangle himself" (his words). He was hesitant. Very hesitant. Still, the urgency of the situation helped her cause, and soon enough he gave the hangar attendant a green light and verbally assented for Ben to fly Harry's plane up to Maplewood.

Bo was proud of herself for once. She helped her family in a huge way. In her life, Bo was typically the family member who needed help. Either she was in trouble and needed bailing out of some sort (never from jail, though!) or she was short on cash or she made an enemy and begged one of her brothers to stand up for her honor (spoiler: they agreed only once- in seventh grade). But now... now *Bo* was the one who came through in a pinch. A very serious pinch. She supposed she had better repay Harry for acting as her crucial accomplice in the matter.

Chapter 7: Ben

Sadly, Ben and Erica were kind of on the same page. Sure, her declaration that morning shocked him, but it validated his own ideas about where things were heading. Or ought to head.

But right now, none of that mattered. He had to get to Maplewood before... well, he didn't want to think about that. Dad would pull through. He was a Stevens. Tough Maplewood stock with longevity coursing through his veins, no matter how much air was trapped inside of them.

Ben cleared his throat, trying to overcome the growing lump as he pictured his father laid up in a curtained-off section of the ICU, wires threaded around him, a machine beeping nearby. His sisters demanding more attention from the nurses, despite the likelihood that he was either in surgery at the hands of a doctor or stable enough to require little attention at all. He could see his mom with her graying hair and dated clothes there beside the bed praying the rosary, probably a blubbering mess.

Now, *that* was true love. People who had been through it all. Four kids. A failing ranch. Pushed into joining the workforce when things got tight. And they made it out. His parents weren't necessarily affectionate folks, but their love was obvious to everyone. Ben shook his head at the thought of disappointing them. Everyone was so proud of the life Ben and Erica had made together outside of Maplewood.

Maybe Erica was right. Everything *was* perfect for a while. He was pinching himself on a daily basis. Ben Stevens, Maplewood High MVP for two seasons, region All-Star, NMU's MVP for four seasons, interest from NFL scouts... even with the onslaught of praise, he had never imagined that his prowess on the field would turn into a lucrative career. One in which he got to travel the country and take good care of his growing family without the brutalization on his body. It was too good to be true.

Then Erica decided she wanted another child. She desperately needed a girl. Luke and Nicky weren't enough for her, or so he later accused. At the time, Ben was hesitant but not against it. He didn't care if he had a boy a girl or anything else.

But she cared a lot. Erica grew up with three other girls. *She* was a girl's girl, whatever that meant. She wanted a mini version of herself to bake with, to shop with, to play dress-up with. *The world needs another ME, Ben*, he remembered her joking. They laughed together, no doubt agreeing that it'd be neat for her to enjoy a special mother-daughter bond.

Finally, he agreed. She got pregnant within a few months and was convinced that her dream was coming true.

He tried to keep her down to earth about it all, but she insisted on shopping for girl stuff right away. She planned an over-the-top gender reveal party for the day she hit 15 weeks.

By then, they had started sleeping in separate rooms. She needed lots of sleep, and he couldn't stand her getting up in the middle of the night to chomp on heartburn pills and use the bathroom. They had stopped going to galas and events together. She lost interest, focusing her free time on admiring Nicky and Luke, mourning the near future when "they'd have to share her with a second little Stevens woman." She'd even allowed her gym membership to lapse, which was crazy. Everything just went downhill in the matter of a couple months. Erica was so consumed with her baby girl- or the idea of her. By the end, Ben was outright pissed off about it all. What was so wrong with having boys, anyway? What was so wrong with their perfect life before that... madness?

Then, Erica woke up one day and told him everything felt off. He didn't give it much thought, since she was still within the first trimester. But then, over decaf coffee, she said the one thing that continued to haunt him: "*I just feel like she's gone.*"

Ben snapped back to present, doing his best to avoid the memory all together.

He had never flown this route and only had a vague sense of the flight path, so he directed Erica to pull the aeronautical map from her dash and help him navigate. He knew if he followed the San Xavier River, it would connect him to the Apache Reservation that stretched from the foot of the Maplewood Mountains all the way to town.

But he would need help navigating over the reservation. It wasn't as simple as heading northeast. Once they hit the forest, it could be easy to get lost over the miles of monotonous trees.

"I want to make sure this spits us out where I think it will, and from there I need to have a sense of if we are moving north or northeast and at what degree." he explained to her.

"Okay, so what do you need me to tell you?" her voice crackled into his headphone. He glanced in her direction, watching her squint through dark lashes as she tried to make sense of the map. She made for a crappy copilot, but she was... cute, he couldn't totally ignore that. Then he remembered the D word, and his lips fell into a frown.

"Here, I'll take that." He grabbed the creased paper and pressed it onto the dash, finding his place with his index finger. "We're here, see?" he raised his voice, but she didn't flinch. Instead, her eyes narrowed onto the paper and she nodded solemnly. "It's easy for me to follow along the river. Look down," he directed.

She leaned to her window, careful of not shifting her weight too hastily. He watched her look over and down beneath them. The red nails of her left hand gripped her seat, and her right hand clenched over her seatbelt. He couldn't help stealing a glance at her smooth, tanned thigh. Erica typically dressed more... event-appropriate, but he knew she'd had no plans for the day. She certainly wasn't prepared for a family reunion. A pitiful smile pricked at the corners of his mouth.

"I had no idea that river was... active?" she called through the mouthpiece. "I figured it was dry this time of year."

"Me either. It's been a dry year. I wouldn't be surprised if it tapers off soon. But for now, it makes it easier for us to keep on the path. Once we hit the rez, I'll need to know exactly which way to point us."

She grabbed the map back from him, determined to help. "It looks like there's another little river or something past the San Xavier that runs straight through the middle of the rez. Maybe we'll see it?"

He looked over at where she pointed and shook his head. "Maybe, but doubtful through the canopy. That's Apache creek. Spits out into Apache Basin, which isn't very big anyway. Even the basin could be hard to spot. By that point, we'll be battling heavy forest topography. Pine trees. Fir trees. Junipers. Oaks.

Full and lush, no doubt. If we can pin down the direction, we'll be fine," he finished before looking back out the front windshield.

The good news was that it was a clear day. The bad news was that he had no working radio, and the plane wasn't exactly in tiptop shape. For starters, it was dirty. The dash boasted a fine layer of dust. The windshield hadn't been cleaned. Trash clogged their footholds. Plus, he wondered what else may not be working if the radio was out.

Chapter 8: Erica

At least they were getting along. The awkward tension lifted somewhat as the two problem-solved around the issue of a defunct radio and Ben's lack of geographical knowledge.

Erica thought back to her sister. She'd heard about this teacher man once before, when she had come out to sign off on purchasing their new home and to bring down some valuables ahead of the move. She stayed with Bo in her dumpy little casita in midtown, but they'd had more fun than Erica dared admit. They got drinks together and went out dancing, and it was the one time Erica felt like she could agree to leave Philly.

The two sisters had ended the night at a Denny's for two-am pancakes. There, they swapped old stories, and Bo mentioned she was taking a course at the community college and she really admired her teacher. It seemed… academic. And totally platonic.

She couldn't remember if Bo had given her a name, and maybe it was a different teacher all together. But ever since Erica had moved to Tucson and Bo began coming up for coffee or dinner, there was no further mention of him. Erica had all but forgotten Bo was even taking a writing class.

Now she leaned back in the cockpit seat, taking a deep breath. She recognized a couple landmarks as they flew over familiar-enough terrain. She hadn't done it often, but when she was a child her family would make a couple trips down to Tucson each year. They could stock up on feed for the animals and sometimes they went back-to-school shopping at the Tucson Mall.

Erica missed those days. Swinging through the clothing racks in Mervyn's Department store as her mother forced her sisters into dumpy denim outfits with Tweety Bird embroidered on the lapels. After what felt like hours of combing clearance racks and rotating between outfits, she would give in and let each daughter pick out her own single outfit, as long as it was on clearance.

After arguing above plastic hangars and red tags, the five girls would meet the boys at CinnAmazing. There, all eight of the Delaneys would share two massive, gooey cinnamon rolls. Erica could smell the sweet buns now as she and Ben sputtered high over a modest hillside peppered in brush and rocks.

Erica then thought of Bo and her rise through the rebel ranks. Once high school had hit, Bo all but turned against her parents entirely. She wore as much black as she could get her hands on. She dated Billy Flanagan, who was a Grade-A Bad Boy and who Dad (and the rest of the town) hated.

Meanwhile, and to Bo's irritation, Erica came into her own, maturing a little ahead of schedule. She never shook her baby-blonde locks, and grew them long, intensifying their white glow by laying out every single day that the thermometer read sixty plus degrees. Playing volleyball and running track kept her toned and svelte, just the way the high school quarterback liked her. She and Ben fell in love in first period freshman year, though years later he admitted he had fallen for her much earlier, in grade school. They'd known each other forever, but something over the summer after eighth grade changed for Erica. Could have been the intangible emotional shift that high school brings. Could have been his burgeoning biceps. Could have been Erica's choice to *not* follow in her wild older sister's footsteps.

But it probably came down to one thing: Ben was a good person. He would become a good man. He reminded her of her father and older brother, and with him she felt safe.

Below them, saguaros began to disappear. Stretches of scrub brush dotted the barren landscape. She felt like, for the first time in a long time, she and Ben were utterly alone. If there was any saving the marriage, maybe this was the time to do it.

"Ben, if you just let me hash some things out, I think we could—" she started but was interrupted by crackling over the radio.

"Harrison Vogel to Piper Cherokee November—"

Erica's eyes lit up, and she flashed a broad smile at Ben, who ignored her.

Her face fell, but her heart picked up a beat. Thank God. It felt better to know that they were in touch with someone.

Ben jabbed the radio button after the static ebbed. "This is Piper Cherokee November 1437 Hotel. Am I speaking to the owner of this plane? Over."

Erica nodded earnestly, mouthing to Ben, "Yes, it's him!"

Static rose and fell over the speaker. Ben uttered a curse, slapping the panel as if to awaken the sleepy radio.

"At least he knows where we are," Erica offered. "Makes me feel safer."

Ben snickered insincerely. "Radio isn't the same as satellite or radar." He hooked a thumb toward the nearly empty compartment behind them. "Every plane flies on radar AND has an ELT beacon. We don't have to be on the radio for the FAA or any other entity to pinpoint us. Don't worry, Erica. Even if I were kidnapping you, the police would track me down quite easily. No. This trip is for my dad, so kindly keep your obnoxious anxiety to yourself."

Erica sank back into her chair, relief flooding through her despite his cold words. She hated flying with Ben, usually. Especially under the circumstances in which they now found themselves. But she had to admit it would be thrilling if he DID kidnap her. Talk about a jolt to the marriage. If only this whole thing *was* a ruse. Maybe Bo and Ben went in on it together, and Ben's dad was totally fine. Healthy. Instead, Ben used it as a trap to lure her away with him to an exotic island off the coast of... well, they were heading north. Okay, lure her away with him to a cozy mountain retreat in Colorado. Heck, at that point she'd settle for Mary's bed-and-breakfast in Maplewood. They could have it out. Work through all their problems and fall back in love. Maybe, by the end of their getaway, things would be different in a *good* way.

Chapter 9: Bo

Harry ended up calling Bo, telling her to come back to La Cienega. He left class early to go home for the day. He wanted to radio in to Ben and Erica to check on them. Bo thought his concern was sweet, so she scrambled back to the airpark, pulling up to his house, which was the first in the development if you went the back way, which Bo always did.

He was stepping out of his car just as she shifted into park. Before she shut off the engine, he jogged over, directing her to keep the engine running. They needed to drive him to the hangar. She did as she was told, waiting for him to pop open the passenger door and slide in. He waved his hand forward without buckling his seatbelt and without saying much more than a hello.

Once inside the hangar, they both noticed the attendant wasn't around. The place was empty. Harry pulled an over-sized bronze key from his pocket and let himself into the control room, or whatever it was called at such a hokey little operation. She stood just outside the room, which fit 1.5 people on a good day, and listened in as he made brief contact with Ben. It was weird hearing her brother-in-law's voice garbled through the rusty speaker system. And, in context of Erica's bold divorce move, everything just felt off. Sad, sure, but more weird.

Now late morning, heat began to appear on the runaway outside: wavy lines forming a distorted puddle of water hovering above the faded spray paint arrows. Bo held her hand to her forehead, wiping the line of sweat that had emerged at her hairline.

Not a moment or so later, Harry descended from the two steps, sighing gravely.

"What's wrong?" she pried, worry creeping into her voice.

Harry walked toward the Caddy, not bothering to wait for Bo to catch up. "Nothing," he grunted over his shoulder. More anxious, she jogged behind him through the dusty parking lot. He pumped the door handle five times before finally allowing her a chance to unlock it. Mildly irritating, but her fear took over.

As they climbed onto the hot leather seats (Ben and Erica were idiots for getting a black vehicle with leather interior in Tucson, Arizona), she kept her gaze on him and paused before starting the engine. "Okay, Harry, let's try that again. I'm going to ask you what's wrong, especially concerning my sister who is on your airplane, and you are going to tell me what's wrong," she demanded again, narrowing her eyes at him.

"His radio's not working. Probably just in an area with a weak signal," he replied, shrinking away from her to prop his elbow on the door as he stared out the windshield.

She swallowed the lump that had begun to form in her throat. "Is the radio structurally crucial to a safe flight?" she joked half-heartedly—whether to still her own worries or assure Harry that she was an easy-going gal, she didn't know. Shaking her head, she pressed the ignition button and backed out of the dusty lot. Relief trickled in as Bo thought more about it: a radio didn't seem like a big deal. Maybe Harry was just unhappy about having someone else fly his plane. She would be unhappy. She was that way, too.

"No, but..." he started, inserting a crooked finger between his teeth and biting down on the knuckle. He flicked a glance to Bo, who twisted her head to him, her blue eyes lasers underneath a furrowed brow.

She had taken her foot off the accelerator, her fear returning. "But what?" she asked, slowly pressing a foot to the brakes and kicking up a puff of powdery dust around the black tank of a car.

Harry shook his head. "Nothing, it's fine. They'll make it without the radio. The plane is fine. No reason to worry. Say, why don't we go back to my place for a bit. Get your mind off your family." A sly smile crept up his cheeks, but, for the first time, Bo wondered if the man she'd come to trust was hiding something important.

She shooed away the thought and drove him back through the ocotillo-lined roads until they pulled up to his burnt-adobe casita. She'd only been there a couple times, but she loved it. It smelled of mesquite and tequila, despite the fact that Harry didn't drink. His Saltillo-tiled floors shone, reflecting in their uneven squares the de Grazia paintings that covered his exposed brick walls. If only one place could represent Tucson, it would be Harrison Vogel's home.

She ran a hand along the back of his worn leather sofa as he went to the kitchen to pour them water. Tucson was always hot in June. But today felt especially brutal. A sinking, exhausting heat that kept her from having any motivation whatsoever. Bo wondered about Ben's dad. She wondered how Erica was going to act in front of his family, knowing what she did.

It occurred to Bo that maybe her little sister would share the divorce idea with their parents or Mary. Unlikely, but possible. Then again, knowing how Erica preferred to keep everyone at an arm's distance in order to preserve the perfect façade she'd built, Bo figured she'd just as soon get the divorce and keep it a total secret. Bo laughed to herself before falling into an over-stuffed armchair and blinking through the sunshine that poured in from floor-to-ceiling windows that acted as Harry's back wall. All that prevented it from falling in on itself was the framing of the sliding glass door that dissected it. Now, as she stared out onto a patio that abutted against earth-tone gravel and carefully designed natural landscape, she realized his view resembled the view from an airplane, except on the ground rather than in the air. It was breathtaking.

"How high is your air conditioning bill to offset that crazy design choice," she joked, pointing to the window.

Harry handed her a sweaty glass of iced water before sitting next to her. "Babe, I, um. I'm leaving town today. I totally forgot to tell you. I have a conference in California. The timing is super crazy and all. What with your brother using the plane, and—"

"Brother-in-law," she inserted, peering up at him over her glass. He stood within an arm's reach, and before he began to drop this bombshell, she was positive he was about to seduce her, right here in plain view of a family of quail as they roped their way through his backyard. She would have turned him down, for sure. Even before he launched into this obvious and strange lie. She would have turned him down.

He stumbled before meeting her gaze. "Right, well. I know this is really out of place, but... let's cool it off for a while, okay? Just until I get back or whatever," he purred as he traced his thumb down the side of her face.

Wait, what? Bo scrunched her face. Was she hearing things? A last minute conference turned break-up? Were they enough of a couple to even call it that? No matter...

She shook her head. "What the hell?"

"No need to yell, jeez." He leaned away, pulling his hand with him as he studied the flagstone fireplace behind her. "My department chair booked this seminar just days ago. I forgot to tell you. We can talk when I'm back. But, I'm going to be out of touch, and I don't need you to worry about me." His voice was sickly soft. Her skin cascaded into goose bumps.

"Where are you going that you can't text? And what about your classes?"

"Subs. Everything's covered. It's a low-tech thing. 'Disconnecting from the Grid and Reconnecting Pen to Page.' You'd love it. Maybe we can go together next time or something."

"Then why hadn't you told me? Are you aware how big of a d-bag you sound like right now?"

He kept his voice even and gazed beyond her still, pretending he hadn't heard her. Or maybe he was just crazy.

"What about my sister and Ben? They have your plane..." She shook her head, totally thrown off. Why had he said nothing about this? And why was Harry suddenly giving off a used car salesman vibe?

"I'm not worried. They'll return it. I trust them," he chuckled before standing himself and brushing invisible lint from his jeans.

As he strode out of the room, leaving her to pace in a desert of confusion, she bit down on her lip, frowning. A new worry hit her like a ton of adobe-freaking-bricks. *Had she made a huge mistake?*

Chapter 10: Ben

"Do you have a water bottle or anything? I'm dying of thirst," Ben asked as they soared over Globe, Arizona and its little fast-food joints and gas stations. He could make out the golden arches of McDonald's easily before they jetted farther north, into an exponentially changing underlay. From highways and town streets framed in rocks and dirt to acres and acres of no roads, but slowly emerging tree-speckled hills.

"No, I have nothing, really," she answered, crossing her arms and looking away out her own window. They'd managed to continue to get along so far, which was a relief. He wondered if that would last once they landed and had to deal with the stress of Dad's situation. Under normal circumstances, he knew she would play it cool. Nothing was more important to her than the outward appearance of perfection and happiness. After a beat, she faced him again. "Don't you hoard Gatorade? I could have sworn you kept IV bags full of the stuff?" The joke fell flat, but she turned and reached an arm to the compartment behind him.

"No," he said, his voice booming in the headset as he threw her a sharp look. "No, I don't have anything. It's fine. We'll be there in about half an hour. She eyed him before shrugging her shoulders and sinking back into her seat.

Once they had passed over Globe, the San Xavier River diverted east toward New Mexico. They were about to reach the reservation, and Ben needed to focus on his coordinates and compass. He'd be useless to his family if he got lost in no-man's land. Plus, they'd need to refuel within forty minutes, at the outermost.

Erica leaned forward and gazed out the front windshield and down over the vast expanse of forest.

"Can you believe we grew up out here?" She was trying to make small talk.

He offered a short nod in response. Ben knew Erica well enough to take a guess at where she might go with this. To him, the moment she asked for the divorce that morning, things changed. Not to say that they wouldn't have to speak to each other again, but why make nice now? Because she thought she could hammer a few more nails into the coffin. That was why. No regard for the fact that his father might be dying as he flew. Did he hate this woman?

A beat passed before she continued, surprising him at first. "I was so excited when we found out about your scholarship. I knew it was going to take us out of this place and somewhere great. I didn't know how great it could even be. I'll always cherish our time in Philadelphia, Ben," she crackled through the headset, any softness in her voice completely sucked out by the engine. But the words weren't soft, anyway. They were passive aggressive. *Why did you drag us away from Philly.* And *Things were so perfect.* And *You ruined my life.*

He could ignore her. He *should* ignore her. But she knew what buttons to press.

"Things could have been perfect in Tucson, Erica." There. Need he say more?

"Well, maybe if you had first handled your business with me, they could. But you decided the best way to deal with tragedy was to uproot your entire family and ignore the hard stuff."

His neck grew hot, and his back began to prickle in sweat again, despite the temperature drop. Brush and shrubs had long ago become towering trees beneath them, and those trees had turned to thick forest. He focused on the compass and took a deep breath, trying hard to ignore the onslaught.

Her voice dropped an octave as she threw a true curveball. "Are we really just going to Maplewood?"

Huh?

He turned to face her. "What? What are you talking about?"

"I thought," she stopped herself before turning away. "Never mind."

"Did you think this was all a ruse and that I was taking you back to your brownstone tower in Philly?" He snorted, and the snort became a laugh. She was delusional. Totally and utterly delusional. He didn't bother correcting her and instead adjusted himself in the seat, stretching his neck and then cracking his knuckles, one by one. What a nutcase.

"No, that's not what I thought. But, I guess," her voice grew louder and she shifted heavily in her seat, lifting her entire body up, despite her seatbelt, in order to fully face him. The plane tilted left as she did so. It didn't matter that Erica weighed 130 pounds soaking wet, any big movement would affect their stability.

Whether to lighten the mood or distract her or make her feel bad about herself or simply cope with the insane amount of stress he was feeling, something in him snapped, and he unleashed a mean joke through the side of his mouth. "Whoa there, big girl!" But he was a stupid man. It did not lighten the mood. It did not distract her. It did not make him feel better or better able to cope. It did nothing more than have the effect of escalating growing tension.

"You freaking butthole, Ben Stevens!" Erica all-out shouted into the headset, and as Ben turned to frown at her and remind her it was just a dumb joke, she cocked her fist back.

Instinctively, he ducked, causing the plane to tilt left nearly ninety degrees.

"Dammit!" he yelled, righting himself before pulling back on the control wheel first. It took a few moments to slowly bring the plane back to position, but they'd jerked so low, they weren't far above the trees, almost skimming the tops, even.

She let out a cackle as if pulling back to deck him was a joke. He was going to handle this woman here and now, and so he kept the plane at the low altitude in order to read her the riot act.

"Are you crazy!" He shouted, turning to Erica, ready to light her up for good.

Erica had dropped her fist, but her face was white as she stared straight ahead. Before Ben could turn his head fast enough, she screamed. A screeching, eardrum-piercing, animal noise blasting from her lips.

And then, deafening silence.

Chapter 11: Erica

She came to in the cockpit, sticky with blood. The entire dash was covered in it too, along with feathers and shards of shattered Plexiglas. She began to test her arms for injury when she remembered where she was.

Ben.

She whipped her head to the left, pain shooting through her back and neck. His eyes were closed and his head hung low onto his chest.

Ben.

"Ben," she finally whispered, croaking like a frog. Fear and nerves buzzed through her like flies. Her heart raced and she swallowed, trying again. A little louder. "*Ben.*"

Nothing.

Oh my God. He can't be dead. Oh my God.

Aching, she unlatched her seatbelt, carefully brushing Plexiglas off her lap, her hands shaking, mouth dry. She rubbed damp hair from her forehead and pulled a feather from her lip, gagging.

Stumbling in the shallow compartment, she hunched over her husband and put her face up against his, listening before holding her fingertips to his neck with one hand and gently tilting his head upright with the other.

Yes, thank God. He had a pulse. A slow but vivid pulse. She leaned back examining his face. It, too, was covered in blood and she had no idea if it was his own or the apparent bird's. Or hers, for that matter. Red splashed throughout the cockpit, erratically, like a crime scene. She swallowed again before returning her head to his, her mouth pressed near to his ear. "*Ben, wake up, baby.*"

She grabbed for the headset that had been slapped back off her ears and pressed the radio button to get a signal. Hopeful, she tried every channel.

"Come in, come in? This is Erica… Stevens. Mayday? May day? Plane down." Had the situation not been dire, she'd have seen the humor in it. She was a total goof, having no clue what lingo to use. But it wasn't funny. A shiver coursed through her and a lump formed in her throat. "Come in, come in. Anybody, please. MAYDAY, OVER!" She squawked through the lump, glancing frantically through the blown-out windshield to get her bearings.

Nothing. After several minutes of testing each frequency and every knob, she returned her attention to her husband, who hadn't even stirred at her piercing outburst.

He was out cold.

Pain vibrated in her neck as Erica glanced around the cabin and out through the gaping hole in front of her. They were on the forest bed, heavy trees closing in on them. The airplane had landed down at an angle, though not sharp. They would have nose-dived if she hadn't grabbed for the throttle, pulling aimlessly up before she, too, passed out. Physically, she was mostly fine. She wasn't sure if she'd lost consciousness from shock or from the landing or altitude or what. She wasn't sure of a lot of things, right then.

She'd seen the bird for at least a second before they'd struck it. It was massive. Scary-looking, too. Now, as she shakily rubbed crust from her eyes and took a closer look inside the tight space, she saw it, there, on Ben's lap. A massive hawk, cracked and bloody. Erica swallowed a wave of nausea. She'd only ever heard of birds getting sucked into engines on take-off. Never of one crashing through a windshield. Was this even real?

Her mind flicked to Nicky and Luke, back at home, at their little day camp. She never should have sent them. She could have had all this time to play with them, take them to the movies or the zoo. Shame on her. The tears came in a rush, her chest heaving with sudden, all-consuming sobs. She swore right then and there that the moment she returned she would grab her two boys and never let go. Come August, she'd volunteer in their new school every day. She'd give up any notions of going back for her degree. They'd become her only focus. She'd coach their little league team. She'd be better than she had been.

By the time it occurred to her that she'd have to move the damn bird to get Ben out, she began to vomit. Violently. Until dry heaves wracked her body, acid stung her throat, and leftover tears streamed down her face. It was all too much. But, at least they were alive. For now.

Quelling the compulsion to gag again, she shoved the leaden animal onto the floor and straddled Ben, reaching on his right side where she fumbled for the buckle before releasing his body from the synthetic strap. As she untangled him, his weight fell forward, pinning her against the dash. Instead of pushing him back, she pawed with her right arm until she found the door latch.

Working it open must have taken over a minute. Her neck hurt so badly. Her arm numb. She realized she needed to change tactics. She wrapped her arms around Ben, one hand cupping the back of his head as though he were a baby (she knew it was a risk to move him, but with his head flopped forward, it would be better to get him flat), and leaned him across the narrow aisle between the seats so that his shoulders and head rested on her seat.

Then, having more room on that side, she worked her door open and hopped down onto the soft blanket of pine needles below. She looked around her, wondering if maybe they had the terrific luck of landing near a remote cabin or even a defunct gas station. But all she saw were miles of trees, some standing, some felled. A surprisingly tranquility enveloped her, and she leaned back up to the plane, assessing how to safely move Ben down.

Ridiculously, an old memory came back to her just then. Something from ten years before.

They had been living together but hadn't yet married. In their little apartment, the young lovebirds snuggled on the couch, watching *Backdraft*. She poked him in the rib and told him it would be smart if they practiced emergency protocol together. Mouth-to-mouth, CPR, and so forth. He laughed her off, but she made him play along. She went first, dragging his heavy body off the couch as he played dead. Once she had him on the floor, pretend CPR turned into a real-life make-out session before he declared it was his turn. Laughing, he slung her effortlessly over his shoulder and tickled her the whole way to bed. It was childish bliss. It was true love.

A sob now escaped her lips as she studied his limp body, slumping down between the seats.

Based on her own neck pain, it was more than likely he had serious whiplash at the least, and she knew that technically she shouldn't have moved him, after all. *Stupid, stupid Erica.*

"Dammit!" she screamed through clenched fists.

Breathing deeply, she weighed her options, looking about the interior of the plane for an answer. It was clear that some of the blood must have been the bird. Some for sure was Ben's, since it crashed through his side of the window and smacked his face, and a cut above his eyebrow was now actively oozing despite his prone position.

That wasn't all. The Plexiglas had done its job of slicing his face and arms, leaving behind hash marks. Some of the splatter possibly came from the cuts she'd sustained from shattered glass, which weren't many but were now stinging as she held herself up against the passenger door frame. Other than those cuts and her neck-ache, she felt surprisingly okay. Not great. But okay. She dared not think what may have happened had she not grabbed for the throttle in time.

Erica bit down on her lip and considered leaving him there in that position but soon realized the weight of his lower half would be pulling on his back and neck. She needed to get him flat quickly. The best route would be to pull him from the plane and onto the earth below. She prayed she wouldn't have to move him again. That'd he'd come to. But if night fell before help arrived, she may have to.

Frowning at Ben's bloodied face, she thought it through. Yes. She could better help him if they were outside of the plane.

She had to pull him out and hope that someone would find them before a predator did. After all, what were the chances they would actually end up out there for days? Slim. Bo knew their flight path. Ben's family did, since he likely told them he was en route. Harrison Vogel also knew their flight plan and maybe he even logged it. Plus there was that signal beacon thing Ben had referred to.

A rescue team would show up within a few hours. Erica had no doubt.

Chapter 12: Bo

She was floored. Not sad, exactly. More angry. Had this loser of a *community college TEACHER* just *dumped* her? To go out of town?

Something didn't add up. Sure, it wasn't like they were "official," and even *she* was hesitant about so much as kissing, but he had no cause to just end it.

Whatever.

Screw him. She didn't need that kind of drama in her life. He was weird anyway. He didn't take his job seriously. She was a better writer than he. A better kisser, too.

Bo was pretty good about dealing with these things. She moved on easily. Maybe too easily.

She had left his house right away and sat in the Caddy as she watched Harry fumble with his keys and stroll lazily toward his own vehicle. Before he noticed her still sitting there at the curb, she secretly flashed him the bird before revving the engine and peeling out, dust kicking up behind her. She hoped he'd have an asthma attack and choke on it.

Bo had to admit… she liked the drama, regardless whether she looked like a teenager the whole time.

Once she was out of the airpark, she doubled back to the shopping plaza she'd just left in order to grab a bite to eat before killing more time before picking up the kids.

A few hours later, she idled at the curb as adorable little cherubs poured from the mouth of the family center at her sister's church. Bo thought about herself having kids one day, but the idea just didn't seem to want to stick. Maybe she and her sister Anna had more in common than just rebellion. Maybe they'd end up child-free together. Spinster sisters with cats, eating tapioca as they watched JEOPARDY! Sounded quite nice, actually.

Although, Anna *was* seriously dating a single dad now, which meant she was either a fraud OR, as their parents would say, had finally come around.

Bo just didn't want to come around.

Once she saw the tow-headed twins bob their way down the walk, she hopped out, pulling up on her jeans and down on her top, and cornered the Caddy to open the door and help them in.

"Aunt Bo, why are you here?" Nicky called from nearly 25 yards away. Luke squinted at her from his side, a frown settling on his little mouth. Nicky and Luke didn't bother with niceties. They got down to business. She liked that about them.

After a short ride home during which she explained that Papaw Stevens was sick, Bo realized for the first time that she'd be staying the night with them. For some reason, she hadn't thought that far ahead. She'd have to make dinner, see about a bedtime routine, and probably borrow Erica's pajamas.

She needed to have an idea about some things, so she pulled her phone to check for messages or missed calls from either of the Stevens, knowing full well that both were probably still mad at her for arranging that Erica join Ben. No matter, she had zero idea about basic things like bath water temperature, toilet stuff (was she going to have to wipe butts?), could the boys drink coffee?, and so forth.

But, all she had missed was a brief text from Mary.

Weren't Erica and Ben coming this morning?

Bo stopped, mid-pancake flip, as the boys bickered over a toy in the background.

Yeah. They flew up this AM, she replied. She knew Mary was unaware of the current state of the Stevens marriage, and Mary likely assumed Erica would be in touch right away.

But Bo knew better. Erica may not even reach out to her own family at all. She had a secret to keep.

She assuaged Mary's worries: *I'm sure they drove straight to the hospital. You saw Vicki Stevens' post. It wasn't looking good. Try not to bug them.*

Bo could practically feel Mary bristle on the other end. If she were on the phone, Mary would whine that she wasn't bugging them, just worried. Mary always worried. About everything. Most of the family had come to tune her out.

Bo decided she'd wait until morning to try and get in touch again. She could manage one night with the two little Stevens animals. Mary could worry all she wanted, Bo was maybe more content than she had been in a long, long time.

Chapter 13: Ben

"Where am I?"

He started to lift his torso but pain shot up his back and into the base of head, which he realized was throbbing, too. He squinted through the headache, and Erica came into view. A forest canopy glowed around her face as she pressed her lips against his head in response.

What? Had his crappy morning been nothing more than a migraine-inducing nightmare? But why was he outside?

"Ben," she breathed out as she leaned away to study his face. "Don't move," she directed and positioned herself, cross-legged, by his head. "Don't you remember?"

He blinked through the light cutting in from foliage above and tried to focus on his wife. Slowly, his vision cleared.

"You're bleeding?" It came out as a question. Everything was a question, at first. And then, like a freight train moving in, it hit him. They were flying to Maplewood. His dad. Still confused, he asked, "Are the boys okay? Why are you bleeding?"

She didn't bother to wipe the crusted red from her face but instead blinked out a tear.

"Ben, we crashed in the woods. The plane went down," she answered, her eyebrows furrowed, mouth trembling.

He lifted his head, the jerking motion sending a knife down his back, then grunted through gritted teeth and pushed himself up. He waved her off as she tried to steady him.

Panting and wincing through unbelievable discomfort, he searched around himself for the plane, finding it behind him, angled down into the earth.

How did they survive?

As if reading his mind, Erica chimed in. "We were flying low, remember? I think the treetops broke our landing, somewhat. But I pulled on the throttle, so we didn't nosedive. It was a bird. A hawk, I'm pretty sure. Came right through the windshield. It was so scary, Ben." She began to sob, short choking sobs. Ben had seen Erica cry maybe twice ever. The memory of the divorce idea clouding his judgment, he wiped a hand across his face, pausing at each tender cut to test its severity. After finding assurance that the worst was just above his eyebrow and more of a bruised bump than a gash, he stared blankly around himself for a moment.

Dammit. "Are you okay?" he asked, at last, giving her a once-over with his eyes. Dried blood speckled her face, neck, chest, arms, and thighs. Running a hand along his forehead again to soothe the throbbing, he pressed his thumb beneath his brow bones. Both eyes were swollen and tender.

Erica shifted her weight back and pushed herself up from the ground, crossing her arms over her chest as she swallowed a final hiccoughing sob. "No. Yes." She paused, and then, "I'm scared."

He licked his lips, drawing a hand to find fresh blood at the corner of his mouth.

"Okay," he replied before slowing pushing up despite the cramping of his neck and back. Had to be whiplash. Brutal. But he could walk, and that's what mattered right now.

"Don't be scared. It'll be fine. We're close to Maplewood. Surely we've pinged and Maplewood Regional has spotted us on satellite by now. How long has it been since we went down?" As he walked back to the wreckage, he turned his head to note the sun had fallen fairly low. It was late afternoon. Very late. *What time had they left Tucson?* His thinking was still foggy.

"I don't know. A long time. I left you for a bit to see if I could get a sense of where we were. It's just forest. For miles it feels like. I think you've been out for a few hours, maybe?" She shielded her eyes and glanced back at the setting sun, too, shivering as its round edge turned fuzzy before their eyes.

As he hoisted himself into the cockpit, he assured her that enough time had passed that by now a search team was certainly en route. Gingerly, he reached for the fallen headset and tested out the radio before remembering it hadn't worked the whole flight. Now, he wasn't even getting static. He tested the panel. Nothing. The battery must have died. *Great.*

He pulled himself into his seat and took a look at the compass. The nose of the plane pointed northeast. So, the crash hadn't really affected their direction, which was helpful. He was fairly certain that if they had to, they could just walk north until they came across Maplewood Highway. The only problem being that they were on the rez, which was massive. Erica was right. Trees for miles. It would take a while.

He called for her to join him at the plane.

"Yeah?" she answered, picking over logs and mounds of pine needles and across the short distance.

"We just need to hang tight. Choppers should be flying overhead within an hour or so. I'm sure of it."

She pulled her hair back, sliding it easily into a rubber band and licking her lips.

"Okay, good. Thank God."

He gave her a hard look, to which she responded with a solemn nod. A silent understanding creased between them. After a beat, she turned around and strode off to a nearby boulder where she perched like a cracked porcelain doll, her glass cuts glowing from afar.

"Erica, you didn't check my bag? Here!" he yelled to her as he twisted back to grab his duffle. His back cracked, and the sharp pain diverted to his left shoulder, settling there as Ben bit down hard on his lower lip, muttering a curse. From the bag, he drew a fresh Gatorade, untouched yet. He had one more in there, which he'd save.

Just in case.

"I though you didn't have anything with you?" she asked, frowning as she strode back up to the aircraft and grabbed for the drink.

"Yeah, well. I lied."

She wrinkled her eyebrows, sipping a bird's share of the sweet liquid, clearly expecting him to explain himself. When he didn't she shrugged and turned away, returning into the forest, as though it was her new refuge.

"Erica," he called after her again, growing more irritated every time she stalked away from him.

"Gotta hit the ladies' room, be right back," she replied over her shoulder, sashaying her hips as she went.

"Is your phone dead, too?" he hollered back.

"Yep!"

Chapter 14: Erica

When he first woke up, she knew immediately that he hadn't remembered about the "D" word. She wanted to throw up all over again. To take it all back. She wanted to return to when they were happy and tsk herself for being such a brat about the whole baby thing. If she had only willed herself to be happy enough with what they had, then they'd still have it. Shame on her.

Here they were, in the middle of what could be a dangerous situation. Well, it already was a dangerous situation. Ben had blacked out for half a day. They were both cut up. Had no food or clothes to shelter them as night drew closer.

She thought about the boys. How scared they would be. They were intuitive, like her. Even if Bo did a great job of assuring them their parents were safe—maybe she even lied by omission and said nothing other than Ben and Erica went to Maplewood for a couple days—they'd still know something was off.

Mary would be freaking out, for sure. She was such a worrywart. It typically irritated everyone, but Erica was thankful for her little sister's anxiety right now. She'd surely press the officials to be expedient. Of course, so would everyone in both the Stevens and Delaney families. *Everyone* was probably freaking out. Not just Mary.

Erica swallowed hard and stole a glance toward the plane while she went about her business. Fortunately, growing up in the mountains had made her into a mountain girl, no matter how far she had strayed. She could squat and pee like a pro, no toilet paper necessary. She watched from her little nature toilet as Ben fiddled with dials and continued to try and get the stupid radio to work.

That was another thing. Erica needed to have a serious talk with Bo about dumping that loser Harrison, if they were in fact dating. Gross.

She finished her business and pulled up her spandex, cringing and wishing she'd dressed better. Oh well. Their accident was, in fact, nothing compared to

Ben's dad's situation. She thought about Papaw Stevens. Erica was scared for him. Scared for Ben. For the boys. Now, as she made her way back to the clearing, she trained her focus on her husband, who had to be reeling with pain. He pressed ahead, not bothering to tend to his wounds. Nothing new there. He wouldn't even let her touch him, much less help him.

And yet, that very quality was one of the things that drove her wild. Ben had always been tough as tar. He never got hurt, and if he did, no one would know. He hid it well. He worked through the pain masterfully.

As she watched him through the empty frame where the windshield once was, she saw the twins. The stubborn little boy in him, biting down on his lower lip and frowning into the dash, his dark, close-cropped hair, his brooding eyes beneath heavy brows. No matter how much she had come to dislike him, she still loved him. The father of her children. Her husband. For now, anyways.

A chill coursed through her just then and she turned in time to face a light breeze as it twisted through the tall trees. As they left Tucson, both were sweating through their clothes, the skin of her thighs sticking to the leather seat beneath her. She knew full well that Maplewood was a solid twenty degrees cooler than Tucson on any given day. Which meant, too, that it would be twenty degrees cooler at night. She wrapped her arms around herself again, crossing slowly over stumps and felled logs as pine needles pricked through her gladiator sandals, back toward the plane.

She shivered again as she pulled up to a stop at the passenger side.

"Why'd you lie about not having anything to drink?" she asked, genuinely curious. Ben never lied. He hardly ever fibbed. He was a straight shooter.

He blew a sigh out of his mouth. "I'm not arguing right now, Erica. It's getting late, and," he stopped, mid-sentence, his eyebrows falling down low as he frowned.

"Wha-?" she began, but he held up a hand and shushed her.

"Shh!"

She stopped, her face wrinkled in irritation at first. Then, as she, too heard it, her eyes and mouth softened, her jaw falling open.

Ben scrambled out of his seat and dashed around to the nose of the plane which was tucked like a lazy lawn dart into a shallow blanket of pine needles.

She jogged backward, craning her neck to look up in time to catch an airplane fly overhead.

And off, past them, into the sinking sun.

DARKNESS FINALLY COVERED them. They estimated it was seven-thirty or eight o'clock and decided to try and keep better track of time. Once the plane scooted across the sky, fear set in. But, Ben was reasonable. And surprisingly helpful. He promised her that by the next day if they hadn't been rescued, they'd start walking to Maplewood. It wouldn't be more than a dozen miles. Actually, it wouldn't be a bad walk at all. They'd make it easily by sunset, he argued.

It made Erica feel better, temporarily. Good enough to agree with him that they'd better try to just rest.

She was starving, though. And thirsty, which was hilarious to her because on any normal day she literally drank no water. She'd have her coffee, iced tea with lunch, and Diet Coke for dinner. Sure, she may be *wearing* gym clothes, but that didn't mean she subscribed to a healthy lifestyle.

Now, here she was, at the end of a day during which she actually did *less* than what she did on a normal day, and she was dying of thirst. It was her mind tricking her. She was only thirsty because she couldn't drink much. As for the eating part, she could deal with that for one night. No issue.

Before giving in to sleeping in the plane, Erica insisted they tidy it up. After all, the dead bird was rotting on the floor of cockpit, seeping in and smelling it up.

Ben put one hand on his hip, the other pointing to the poor beast. "I'm the one who was *hit* by the bird, Erica. You take it out."

She looked at him, eyebrows cocked, her mouth hanging open, *not* because she was one of those girls who couldn't stand bugs (she didn't mind any of that-bugs, animals, dirt, whatever). But because Ben had *always* been chivalrous. He even pretended Erica minded gross stuff and would take on the job of removing spiders from the house or, more recently, skimming dead rats out of their pool with a mock brave expression. He loved being the *man*.

She closed her mouth, realizing this was the result of the divorce idea. In her head, it was still just an idea: a half-baked one. It was becoming clear, however, that he had taken it one hundred percent seriously. They were getting a divorce. As she pushed past him and leaned down to grab the bird by its clammy, rigor mortis feet, Ben laughed behind her. Actually laughed.

She turned to him, confusion sweeping her face ahead of a small smile.

He grabbed her arm and pulled it back out of the cabin, his laughter fading and face turning somber again. "I was just kidding. I've got it, Erica. Why don't you go clean up your side."

She felt emotional all over again, nodding her head and smiling up at him, hoping he could see the apology in her eyes.

Erica tried to make light conversation, at first asking Ben if he wanted to make a bet about what time tonight a search party would find them. It was something they did all the time: made small bets on silly things. *Winner get a full body massage!* Or *loser has to streak around the background!* It was a small couple's habit she'd loved.

His reply to the idea was a callous joke. "Winner gets to keep the house?"

If they weren't actually maybe getting a divorce, she'd probably crack up. But they were. So, it was a slap to the face. But she deserved it.

Still, she pressed ahead, refusing to let anger or worry consume her. She ignored the dig and chattered away, proposing scenarios about what the boys might be doing with Bo. "Maybe they're playing a board game? Or making cookies?"

Again, he was cruel in his answer. "I just hope we can trust her to keep them alive. Because obviously your sister has awful judgment."

Though Harrison Vogel wasn't the reason the plane crashed, she saw his point. No way was she going to agree with him, though. She was done playing nice for now. Sinking into her own worry would be better than trying to make amends only to be shot down over and again.

If it was even possible, the night sky grew darker, clouds crossing beneath the stars, and they hunkered down in the plane, Ben propping himself up in his seat, Erica asking him to join her on the floor in back, *just for warmth*.

He wouldn't. He couldn't, he said. She hoped, in part, that he was just going to play lookout, rather than carry on in his hatred of her so much that he'd forgo warmth on a chilly night just so he could avoid touching her.

Chapter 15: Bo

Bo couldn't sleep. She wasn't sure if it was the fact that she was in someone else's bed or the unforeseen events with Harry. So, in the early dawn hours, she finally gave up and decided to pull her phone from its tether at the side table. Thank God Erica had the same model, since Bo never packed her charger and hadn't had a chance to go home. She made a mental note about letting Mary know Erica's phone was probably dead.

Bo woke her own device and began to scan, dipping in and out of her various social media and news apps. While scrolling aimlessly through, she nearly passed a photo posted by Ben's sister, Vicki. Bo thumbed the image, bringing it to full screen.

There lay Ben's dad, eyes closed, breathing machine pumping air into his nose. He was still alive. *Thank God*, Bo muttered. She tucked away the good news for when the boys awoke. Of course, who knew how things may play out, but for now it seemed that everything in everyone else's life was okay. It made Bo realize how out-of-whack her own life was. The thought pushed her down deeper into the warm comforter in the gorgeous house with the adorable boys where she had found some temporary comfort and happiness.

Sure, she still (barely) had her gig with the paper. But now the guy she thought of as her boyfriend had ditched her without so much as a goodbye. Meanwhile, she was still entangled with him because her sister borrowed his plane for a family emergency. So it'd be fun to have to reunite with him once they returned. Bo wasn't looking forward to that.

As for anything else in her life? Well, there was nothing. She had no pets. She rented her apartment and did a poor job of that, if the fact that she had to start budgeting for a monthly late fee was any indicator. Friends? She had none. Unless you counted sisters, which Bo hardly did. They weren't friends if they had no choice in the matter. In fact, sisters were more like hostages, really.

Sadly, Bo realized Erica was the only other person she even really talked to, and that was only because Erica moved to Tucson. She was stuck with Bo. Mary and Anna were like distant relatives, getting in touch only when they needed help or when she needed help.

As if on cue, a new message flashed down from the top of her screen. It was Anna. *Speaking of useless sisters*, Bo thought to herself. She clicked open the message, curious.

Mary's freaking out. Have you heard from Erica or Ben?

Realizing she had no sense of what time it was, Bo glanced up at the clock on her phone screen. 4:30. Maybe she *had* slept. She must have misread the digits when she first clicked her phone on, because she could have sworn it was much earlier.

She put together a quick reply.

No, but she left her cell charger here. Phone's probably dead. I'm sure they're still at the hospital. If Mary is so worried then she ought to drive down there herself.

There, that would put an end to it.

K thx.

Bo rolled her eyes. Nice talking to you, too, Anna.

Just then, the bedroom door slowly cracked open, startling her. Confused and panicked, she sat up, her phone crashing to the floor.

"*Who's there?*" She hissed into the darkness.

Two miniature shadows filled the gap of the door. Bo clutched her chest and forced herself to let out a breath.

"What are you guys doing awake? You scared the bejeezus out of me," she whispered.

"We're scared, Aunt Bo," one of the two cried softly. She had no idea which was which. Erica's blackout curtains did their job, as did the long hallway that preceded her private suite.

She squinted through the blackness and threw back the comforter. "Get over here and snuggle with me, you two," she commanded of the pair before they swiftly bounded onto the king-sized bed and wiggled their way in on her left side.

She inhaled their early morning boy scent, catching a whiff of fabric softener as they hunkered under the covers and shut their eyes. Their warm little bodies soothed Bo back to sleep. Maybe Bo and Anna had both been wrong.

Maybe kids weren't so bad after all.

Chapter 16: Ben

Ben was surprised at how well Erica was handling the situation. Then again, no he wasn't. She'd always been physically tough, even throughout her postpartum grief. A nagging feeling tugged inside his head, as though he was forgetting something. Or on the brink of remembering it, but nothing came. He shook it away, allowing anxiety to replace the pull.

Logically, Ben knew it took a while to mobilize search parties. And yet sleeping out in the middle of the rez in a downed plane with no windshield felt very... *Lord of the Flies*. Like it would no doubt end badly, even if they were rescued. His mind floated to his dad and his heart sank. Then images of his sons passed into consciousness, serving only to make him feel more upset.

Once the sun had officially set and darkness crawled across the forest floor, he knew something really *was* wrong. He just didn't know what. Erica swore by Bo's questionable "boy friend," even though it should have been obvious from the messy cockpit and faulty radio that he wasn't a particular person.

Ben was a particular person. When he had kept his own Cessna back in Philly, he ran it regularly, ensuring everything was in good working order, and he had it professionally cleaned once a month, regardless of if it had any use. Of course, he could afford that. If a man owned an aircraft, then he could afford to give it a once over every now and again.

What worried him, however, weren't the errant fast food napkins that flew about the compartment as they took off. It wasn't the layer of dust rattling over the dash during ascent. It was the radio. Ben should have taken it as a warning sign. An omen.

Then again, they'd hit a bird. That wasn't Harrison Vogel's fault. It wasn't even Ben's or Erica's fault. The bird was damn bad luck.

But what *was* Harrison's fault was a broken frickin' radio, preventing Ben from making contact with anyone at all. And, Ben worried further, what else might be malfunctioning?

By the time he had convinced Erica it was more or less safe to sleep, he began to wonder, though. On one hand, he assumed it'd be relatively easy for the FAA to locate them as soon as they were aware that the flight plan had failed. On the other, he figured it could be tricky, being that they were embedded deep beneath the forest canopy.

But if a search crew had gotten a ping and knew their general location, at the very least, then why hadn't a single helicopter buzzed by above? All they had seen was an aloof jumbo jet floating overhead, completely unaware of the near-tragedy below. Frantic waving and screaming on both their parts did little more than dry out their throats and intensify his headache.

Once darkness encapsulated them, with nothing overhead except for scattered stars offering no real light, Erica nagged him further.

"You said we'd be rescued by now," she snarled as they climbed into the plane. He could feel her brushing feathers from the seat before she sank down, propping her legs up on the dash.

He sighed. "Obviously I was wrong." He hadn't wanted to go down the "survival" road, mentally, but now that it must be well past eight in the evening, he figured he'd better. At that point, they needed to ensure their own safety, at least for the time being.

"I think we should take shifts," he suggested, searching for Erica's eyes in the twilight.

She was quiet for a beat before replying. "Do you really think either of us will be able to sleep?"

"We should try. There's a small chance we could be out here a little longer. This forest is massive, and they may have a larger search area to work from if we glided for some time. And we definitely glided for a ways, right?"

"So you're saying it would have been better if we had just crashed. If I didn't pull back on the control wheel and save our lives?" Sarcasm dripped from her mouth. He wanted to say that technically, yes. If they had dropped where they were, they wouldn't have fallen off radar, which was highly likely. Something kept him from admitting as much. "And can't we turn on lights in here? It's not like we lost power."

"If we don't need them, then we are leaving them off. It's not like I can take off and fly us home. In case you didn't notice, your brilliant attempt at salvaging the flight became useless when you couldn't land us evenly on the ground." He waved a hand out in front of him. "The damn propeller is busted."

She knew that, but he didn't know how else to communicate with Erica anymore. Their language of love had devolved into continual and useless arguments. Anyway, even if the radio was down and they drifted below radar, they still had the beacon, he was sure.

His eyebrows dropped and a frown pulled at his mouth as the vague reminder to do something nagged at him. It felt within grasp, but exhaustion had begun to envelop him.

"Well, can we at least sleep together on the floor back there?" Erica interrupted his train of thought.

He glanced behind him as if he a dimly lit nook with pillows and comforter would appear out of thin air.

"No thanks. You can move back if you want. I'm fine here," he grunted as his eyes grew heavy.

BEN SWALLOWED HARD in the early morning light as it bled in through the barren windshield. He twisted in his seat to look back at Erica, her eyelids fluttering as she twisted awake on the floor behind him. He thought of the boys and how worried they would be. He thought of his dad. He felt sick. Turning away and running his hands up and down on his arms to warm himself, he muttered, "Good morning."

"I'm freezing. I didn't sleep a wink," she squeaked, sharing the same experience as he. They should have slept together for warmth. He should have joined her on the floor in the back, wrapping her frail, barely clothed body in his. There was no need for a lookout after all. No one came.

But Ben couldn't do it. He wasn't gonna sleep well anyway, and he had no interest in even touching Erica. His ire had quadrupled since the morning before. Maybe hitting the bird wasn't Erica's fault, but her awful admission launched them into this entire disaster.

"Yeah, I know." He rubbed his hands together and opened his door. "I'm gonna go to the bathroom."

He wandered a few feet off and behind a tree to pee, remarking how slowly the sun was rising. Birds overhead chirped to life and rustled through the leaves of tall oaks. It would be a beautiful scene, if not for the circumstances. As he went about his business, he watched Erica descend from the airplane, wobbling, shivering, and making her way to the opposite side of the clearing. Their landing hadn't done much to disrupt the sturdy trees, but it split a few branches and some thinner fir trees bent under the weight of the plane, now lying beneath the dead vessel like a failed hammock under the weight of a sumo wrestler. The whole event left a maze of branches and a modest space for them to move around in, like a child's forest fort.

He licked his lips and wandered back to the plane, pulling out the opened bottle of Gatorade he'd stashed under his seat. Erica had accused him of keeping her from a basic necessity, but he'd argued that it would be smart to ration the fluid, and he had better discipline than she. Of course, that idea nearly sent them in to yet another argument, but he refused to engage and ignored her. Finally, he had coughed up an apology to which she answered that rationing scared her. What did he think? That they'd be out here for days?

He'd cut her off and reminded her of the beacon and that they were directly in the planned flight path. But, as dawn broke and he began to second guess his own assurances, he figured he would need to shift the conversation, no matter how much it frightened her. Or him.

Leaving the cap off, he offered her a sip as she returned from across the clearing.

She threw him a weary look before accepting the still-almost-full bottle. He eyed her as she drew it to her lips before flashing him an insincere smile and passing it back.

He rolled his eyes, screwed the cap back on and then it came to him. He meant to check the beacon. He thought he had. Did he? Once he had come to and assessed the damage to the plane, he was going to check the beacon. Make sure it was there and not damaged.

A sinking feeling welled in his gut and he pushed the bottle to Erica, dashing to the plane to check.

It wasn't there.

There was no beacon.
But he couldn't tell Erica.

Chapter 17: Erica

She wasn't stupid. She had put two-and-two together throughout the night. Rescue had, for some reason, been delayed. She was certain it had nothing to do with her sister. Erica knew her sisters and parents were all beside themselves with worry by now. Not to mention poor Nicky and Luke. She even jumped ahead to her eventual return, wondering if they would be able to get over this whole trauma. This sort of thing could really stick with kids.

She wondered if *she* would get over it. All of this mess. She flashed a glance to Ben, who was fiddling with something. Stubble now peppered his jaw as she watched him bite his thumbnail and smudge dried blood from above his eye. He was so handsome and strong, and she had been ready to let him go. How had their marriage come to this?

"Ben," she leaned against his door, her arm crooked on the window frame.

He didn't look up from his squatting position. "Yeah?"

She bit down on her lip, considering what to say next. How to say it. Finally, almost under her breath, the words came. "I'm sorry."

He didn't react. Her heart stilled, and she tried again. "Ben, I'm sorry about what I said yesterday."

He slapped his hand down, stood, and moved in to grab the map, an odd expression filling his face. "Sorry for what you said because we are stranded alone together? Or sorry because you actually *don't* want a divorce—you just wanted to hurt me by saying the most awful thing in the world?"

She blinked, unready for the heat of his words. The sadness and anger in them. Faltering a moment, she scrambled for an answer. "Both, I guess."

He blew air out his lips and then laughed. A cold, mirthless laugh. "Covering all bases. That's so like you, Erica," he ran his hands through his hair and wiped the map off his lap and onto the console before moving his muscled body down from the seat and squeezing past her. "Time to scout the area," he called back, not waiting.

She had no idea what he meant, but they were stuck together. So, now was as good a time as any to talk it out. She jogged after him, hooking her hand on his left shoulder and tearing it back.

"Talk to me, dammit, Ben." Her voice was firm but not loud. It got his attention. He whipped around.

"Erica, you asked me for a divorce. That's a very final thing. I'm not going to rehash nearly two decades of our relationship. I just won't. You want to talk survival? Fine. I'm happy to talk survival." The words dripped like acid from his lips, but he didn't turn away from her to keep walking. He waited, watching her, his lower lip trembling, almost imperceptibly. It was that little mannerism that told Erica that everything would be okay. That he was scared, too. And not of being... lost out here. But of *losing* her.

She swallowed hard, tears pricking her eyes, and then she fell into him, her arms around his neck, her face pressed along his taut chest. To her great relief, he replied in kind, holding her tightly to him, kissing the top of her head. Her body flooded with warmth, and she relaxed her hold on him, leaning back to see that he was crying, too.

IT WASN'T QUITE A TRUCE. They hadn't made up. But, at least for now, they were on the same team. The tears dried quickly on her rosy cheeks as Erica and Ben looked out into the woods.

Hardly able to stifle her nervous impulse to laugh after the hug and tears and kiss, a warm smile spread across her lips.

"What?" He cocked an eyebrow, wiping at his face and throwing her a sidelong glance.

She answered, "Nothing. Well, I mean... it feels good to hug you. That's all. Anyway. What are we looking for? It's all trees, clearly." She waved her arm in a sweeping gesture.

He blew out a sigh but offered her a small, half-smile. "Well, we gotta decide if we are gonna stay or walk, darlin.'"

She shook her head, the smile fading. "Obviously we stay. We've got the plane. It's how a search crew will find us. Plus, it's shelter, right?" She looked up at him, earnest. Erica was born and raised in these here woods. She knew the basic principles of survival, one of which was to establish shelter. They had that, even if the front windshield was blown out and blood-encrusted.

Propping his hands on his hips, he paused a beat before responding. "That would be true if we were totally lost in the woods."

She laughed. "Ben. We *are* lost in the woods."

Then, he squared his shoulders to her, a shadow of hope crossing his face. "We know where we are. But the, eh, the beacon isn't foolproof, Erica." He averted his eyes before going on. "And anyway, I mean, I think... or rather, I *don't* think we are lost. I think we're only... missing."

Erica shivered. *Missing* sounded a lot scarier than *lost*.

Chapter 18: Bo

It all happened so quickly. The call from Mary unleashed total chaos.

Mary had gone to the hospital. The good news was Ben's dad had come around. He was still in the hospital, but the prognosis was positive.

But the good news was lost on Mary when Vicki Stevens explained that Ben and Erica had never shown up at the hospital. Initially, Mary leapt to the conclusion that they'd somehow learned of his dad's impending recovery. Maybe they decided to take advantage of a romantic getaway? But that notion was squashed by the Stevens family. No one had heard from Ben or Erica. At all.

Mary, smart as she was, made the next logical move. She called Maplewood Regional Airport and demanded to speak to the person in charge.

No, they had not hosted an incoming flight from Tucson. No, they had not been aware of any incoming flight from Tucson.

Or Golden Valley.

Or Globe.

Or anywhere. Their next scheduled intake was for midmorning, a private charter from Albuquerque.

Mary told Bo that she drove to the airport herself to confirm the bad news. Once there, the employees swore up and down that not only had they not been made aware of any Ben Stevens or Harrison Vogel, but they hadn't seen any local activity of a private plane, either.

Dick Delaney and Margaret showed up right after Mary, asking the same questions and receiving the same answers. When Mary explained all this to Bo and Anna, Bo initially considered hiding the fact that Erica had asked Ben for a divorce. It would humiliate Erica for her sister to reveal that news. But then she reasoned it could explain their unexpected absence. Could Ben have... turned on his wife? Bo truly didn't think so, but they were panicked when they left. Maybe he lost it.

Uncertain what to do and in a panic of her own, Bo came clean to everyone via a three-way call between the sisters and parents.

"Were they fighting this morning?" Margaret's voice screeched over the speaker, echoes booming around her, proving to Bo that her mom, dad, and Mary were still at the airport. A sad scene, probably, the three of them standing at some useless Customer Service desk as a nobody employee offered a string of "I don't knows."

Now getting dressed and ready to drive up, Bo exhaled, nostrils flaring. "Well, gee, Mom. I don't know. If you asked Dad for a divorce, do you think he'd be a happy camper?" She felt like she could explode into her mother.

"Roberta, knock it off," her dad's voice came on firmly. She could hear the anger and fear, and it made her throat clench. "How did they seem when they took off? We need to know if we should alert the police. Could Ben have... kidnapped Erica?"

She couldn't help it, she laughed. The very question that occurred to her now seemed utterly ridiculous. She knew for a fact that the answer was no. She said as much but added that they should definitely call the police, anyway. This wasn't a kidnapping, but it was a missing persons.

"I don't know if that makes me feel better or worse," Anna chimed in over the line. Her voice cutting in and out as she went on, "We're driving up from Phoenix now."

Mary's boyfriend, who happened to be Anna's boss, would drive Anna to Maplewood straight away.

Bo would drive herself, and she had no choice but to bring Nicky and Luke.

Mary and the Delaneys would call the police. No matter where Erica and Ben had gone, they were one hundred percent missing.

"WHERE ARE WE GOING, again?" Luke squinted at her through the early morning sun as Bo fastened them into their booster seats. "I can do this myself, Aunt Bo," he slapped her trembling hands away.

Nicky joined in as he tugged the strap across his chest with might, "Yeah we can do it ourselves. Where are we going, Aunt Bo?"

She couldn't ignore the question forever.

"Boys, we're gonna go see your mom and dad, okay?"

She'd expected the car ride to feel like the longest of her life. But the distraction of the twins in back making war sound effects helped to pass the time. She was relieved that they didn't freak out when she (very generally) explained that "we aren't quite sure where they are, so we are going up to the mountains to find them."

Instead of scaring them, the news was a call to action for the tough kids. They schemed the whole way, discussing – in boy talk – how they would hunt the bad guys and camp out in the woods with binoculars. At turns, Bo felt like laughing and crying. She considered every possibility as she wove through winding small towns and crested desert hills as they made their way up, up, up.

Ben and Erica were in an airplane, for goodness' sake. So, if there had been a crash, everyone would know by now. Ben would have radioed at the very least, but even more probable was that they'd been detected by some radar or something by... what was it called? The FCA? FFA? Whatever the entity was that ran air traffic. But, according to hokey little Maplewood Regional, no. No flight came in or was detected. And by now, if there had been a crash, they'd know. News reports blinking across her mind, viral Facebook posts and intrusive messages... Bo could picture it all. *Heard about the plane crash, what happened!* Or *OMG Bo, your sister! Is she okay?!*

None of that, so far. Bo discreetly glanced onto the front passenger seat to ensure her phone had no new alerts.

Nothing.

Then again, Bo had so few friends or even acquaintances. Her Facebook was filled with people who didn't really know her or her family, so maybe there wouldn't be anything. Another thought pushed its way into her head.

Harry.

Earlier, while the family was planning their course of action, Bo shot a few strongly worded texts to the elusive instructor.

No word from Ben or Erica. They never landed. Ppl trying to get in touch with you. Airport, even.

Moments later she tried again:

Where are you?

Seconds after that she tried again:

Call me now. It's your plane. It's an emergency.

She'd have assumed his phone was off, except for the READ receipt she received with each outgoing message. He - or someone - saw the messages.

She'd called, too. No answer. Mary said the airport and police would be tracking him down as well. But if Harrison Vogel thought Bo wouldn't spam him with calls at all hours of the day and night until he gave her the info she needed, he had another thing coming.

Now, as she drove, she decided to try again. Never having connected her phone to Bluetooth, she gave the boys their first military mission assignment.

"Nicky, Luke," she snapped her fingers back at them before tossing the phone onto the middle seat that spread between their little bodies. "I need you to call someone," she commanded.

"Mom?" Nicky trilled in unison with Luke who asked, "Dad?"

"No, neither," her voice cracked, but she adjusted her sunglasses and steadied herself. "Go into the recent calls... can you do that?" She glanced in her rearview mirror to Luke, who was directly behind her.

"Yeah?" his answer came as a question. *Great.*

"Okay, do you see a name that starts with the letter H?" Her voice rose in pitch as she channeled her non-existent, inner preschool teacher.

Nicky chimed in, "Right there, dummy. Look, it says 'Harry.'"

Bo's eyebrows wrinkled with surprise. "You can read?" She looked over her shoulder at the two boys who simply nodded as they studied the phone. *Amazing.* "Okay, call him up, guys," she directed and held her hand back for Luke to return it.

A high-five echoed between the twins as the phone began to ring.

Once.

Twice.

And then, a hushed voice.

"Hey, Bo."

Chapter 19: Ben

Ben licked his lips and considered Erica's point. Staying was smart. He crossed his arms as he took in the immediate area. It was just after sunrise now, rays of early morning light spreading over the forest floor and through the tree trunks. Sure, he was used to getting up before the crack of dawn, but he was amazed by the fact that he didn't feel tired. Not well-rested, but not tired.

Being out there in the woods reminded him, at first, of his dad and brothers. They went camping several times a year. Often to hunt, sometimes just for fun. Sometimes the whole family would join the boys, the girls complaining about being cold or dirty.

His mind wandered forward, and he recalled high school. After a solid two years of dating, he and Erica eventually managed to convince their families to let them go on group (coed) camping trips. Those very trips pushed Ben from crush to full-blown attraction to deep love for the blonde bombshell.

He remembered their first group trip very clearly. It was Erica and him; his brother Steven and Steven's girlfriend, Caroline Zick; and Bo and her boyfriend, Billy Flanagan. By then, Ben and Erica were juniors, a year younger than everyone else. Erica was in her element. She'd brought fresh eggs from the Delaney farm, premixed pancake batter, a cast iron pan, oil, and a crocheted blanket she'd made herself.

Ben felt transported to the 1800s, but Erica wasn't playing house. She was completely and totally herself, masterfully helping to set up the tent and making their bed while bossing the other couples to clean up after themselves. Bo had reminded Erica of her place in the pecking order, but Erica reminded Bo that *class* came before class. Ben had laughed at that and remembered it into the night, as they cuddled together on top of their sleeping bags, the afghan doing little for warmth. It was for discretion and style, Erica had told him. He laughed at that, too. They were camping, after all. She gave him that point, agreeing that nature was stylish by default.

But above everything else on that romantic little trip, what amazed him most was that she never once complained. About anything. At all.

Now, as she rubbed her hands up and down her goose-fleshed arms, he could see that same teenaged girl. Almost everything in the preceding years had made sense to him. Their wedding, small but perfect. Their home in Philadelphia, a far cry from their upbringing. Still perfect. Erica liked to make the most of life, whether she lived it in a brownstone walk-up or out in the sticks. To Erica, the idea of perfection meant that she had control.

And then it clicked. Control. She didn't hate Tucson. She hated that it couldn't save her baby. She didn't hate him. She hated their circumstances. He looked back to the plane, its nose rooted in the ground, and pictured his duffle bag, tucked neatly into the compartment behind his seat. Its contents. Was now the time?

Erica's sweet voice broke his concentration. "Ben? Don't you think?"

He threw a glance her way, her face was flat as she awaited his response.

"Don't I think what?" Then he remembered. "Oh, yeah. Well, if we were totally lost then yeah, we ought to stay. But all we have to do is walk north, and we'll hit the highway within a few hours. A day at the outside," he rubbed his jaw, wondering if he should let her talk about the divorce thing even after him shutting her down for months. Was it too late? Would the thing in the duffle bag even help? Did he even want to go there now that she had used the D word? Honestly, no. She'd burned him pretty damn hard. He should probably just keep it.

Erica cocked her head and answered, "Are you sure we shouldn't wait just a bit longer? Give it another day?"

She had a point, but an image of his father, laid up in a hospital bed, flashed before his eyes. Did he have that kind of time? Likely not. Everything seemed urgent. Waiting a day could pan out, but it could also be a waste. He looked above them, studying the tree tops and assessing visibility. They could stay, try to make a fire, and the smoke may draw attention to rescue choppers. Hell, they could burn down the forest.

No.

Ben's dad didn't have that kind of time. He knew they could make it to town probably before rescue. If he had a shot at seeing his dad, he had to take it. He wasn't going to miss out on a goodbye, if indeed a goodbye had to be said. He blinked away a tear and swallowed hard.

"We're walking. If we are still walking by night, then we'll set up camp- a fire, so forth." There. Decision made.

Erica crossed her arms over her chest. "Ben, come on. That's way riskier. We start a fire here, they're sure to see us even if the beacon thing isn't working. Don't be stupid," she finished. It was all he could do not to leave her there, alone, unaware (still) that there was NO beacon. Didn't she get it? They might lose his dad. He may never see him again. Ben admitted as much.

"What about my dad, Erica? He could be dying right now. He might already be dead," his voice cracked and he raised it higher as he tried to combat the emotions. "I lost my daughter already this year, I can't lose my dad," the last words came out as a staccato whisper and he crumpled down to the ground, crying like a baby.

She rushed down to him, blanketing him in her skin and hair and womanly scent. But he could barely feel her. Hardly tell she was even there.

Chapter 20: Erica

It was everything he ever needed to say. That he felt it too: the deep, all-consuming sadness. That he couldn't let go. If only he had confessed much, much earlier. It might have saved them.

Maybe it still could.

Delicately, she knelt down beside her husband, wrapping him in her arms and tucking her face into his neck. Erica thought about her own regrets, particularly her words the previous morning. But did she really regret them? Did she really not mean it? Could she go on with her life without Ben?

Yes, she could.

Because that's exactly how they'd been living for nearly a year as he sunk himself deeper into his career, leaving her to raise the boys by herself.

To be pregnant *alone*.

To miscarry *alone*.

To grieve *alone*.

To move to Tucson *alone*.

As Erica Stevens let her husband finally mourn in her arms, all she could think of was that word. That feeling. *Alone*.

But for now, she couldn't leave him alone. They needed each other, not just for happiness or day-to-day low grade misery, but maybe for survival. The thought sent chills coursing down her underdressed body.

He must have been reading her mind, because he wiped his face with the backs of his hands and then moved his arms around her, hugging her to him for the second time in less than a day. They hadn't hugged in weeks. Maybe months.

"Erica," Ben whispered through the cool morning air as he pulled away. She fully expected him to take that moment to apologize. *He had enough self-awareness.*

When he didn't go on and instead stared at the plane, she realized there was no apology coming. But, at least he must be considering her idea: set up camp and hunker down in the plane until rescue. She followed his gaze and prompted him. "Yeah?"

"I need my duffle. Walk with me."

Rolling her eyes behind his back, she followed him, as they picked their way over felled logs and through saplings, back to the clearing. Just as they passed around the thick trunk of a juniper, Ben stopped, holding his hand behind him to stop her, too.

"What?" she demanded, craning her neck around him to see why he'd stopped.

He whipped his head back, holding his hand to his mouth to shush her, his eyes ablaze.

Confused still, she chose the tree to lean on rather than Ben's shoulder. She pressed into it, peering around her tall, broad husband. The first thing that occurred to her was, being in such a position, directly behind his left arm and coming up only to his chest, she could smell his deodorant. It amazed her. She wanted to comment on it. *Ben, despite being stuck in the woods for nearly 24 hours, you still smell nice.* It was a miracle. The ridiculous thought passed and she pressed up to the tree again, finally following Ben's steady gaze to the plane.

She whispered up to him, "What?" She didn't see anything. Like a cat, he fell back a step, and covered her mouth with his mannish hand, crouching down to whisper in her ear. When she was thoroughly bewildered and her eyebrows couldn't scrunch any closer together, he pinned her with a severe glare and finally removed his hand to point. She followed his long finger to the far side of the plane.

At last, she saw it.

A slow-moving black bear, its puffy coat trembling about itself as he clawed stupidly at the door of the plane.

Erica's face fell and she looked up to Ben, her eyes in question. *What should they do?*

Silently, he shook his head and then moved his left hand from the tree to the small of her back.

She couldn't tell what was to blame for her skin prickling and blood freezing and heart stopping and pace tripling...

The bear?

Or the feel of Ben's strong hand resting so close to her rear end?

His touch was both old and new. Nostalgic and foreign. Comforting and thrilling.

As she bit down on her lip, she flicked a glance up at him. Deftly, he shifted a step closer, his eyes trained on the bear, his grip repositioning itself directly on her hip bone.

Definitely his hand.

Chapter 21: Bo

"Harry, where the hell are you?" Bo hissed into the receiver, ignoring the boys as they gasped at her language.

His voice was low and clouded in static. Bo was about to leave the town limits of Globe and move into the forest, where she'd have no service. She contemplated pulling over. Harry might have important information. Wasn't it more important that she speak with him than make it to Maplewood to sit around twiddling her thumbs?

Yes.

After checking her rearview and side mirrors, she veered down the next dirt patch to the side of the two-lane highway. Cars and RVs, semis, and motorcycles sped past as she frantically pushed him for information. She didn't want to worry the kids, but she had a feeling this would be the last time she'd ever talk to Harrison Vogel.

After a slew of rapid-fire questions, he answered sheepishly that he really did have a conference. He really was planning to break up with her. His sudden departure wasn't mean to be subversive behavior, but that no, sadly, the plane wasn't in great shape. The radio and panel needed a work up. He had flown the thing recently, but only from La Cienega to Tucson International Airport and back to pick someone up. Bo felt foolish, but it seemed relevant to ask who? When?

"A friend. A couple weeks earlier." Bo's mind flashed back to a clear memory. It was the day after the first time she and Harry spent a night together. He'd left in the morning without so much as a goodbye. But before he had made it to his car, he had to jog back into her sleepy little townhome to grab the phone he'd forgotten.

Bo had read the recent text exchange, because Bo was a journalist. Info digging was her job. He had plans to pick up a "Brittany Purcell" from the airport.

Their texts were all business, awkwardly so, and Harry had convinced Bo that Brittany Purcell was an old friend coming for the weekend.

Bo knew it was more. But she didn't press the matter.

"Brittany Purcell?" she prodded through the phone.

He answered, his voice growing impatient, "Yes, Bo. Brittany Purcell."

She didn't care about Brittany. Instead, she pushed ahead. "Was the plane in working order? Did it have any issues? Harry, this is serious. No one knows where Ben and Erica are. No pings from the plane. No radio, nothing. It's like they fell off the map."

His lame response did nothing to make her feel better. "The plane is fine. Engine works great. No issues. Except the radio. If they crashed, it wasn't my fault," he whined through the phone.

Bo's blood began to boil. "Maybe not if they crashed. But if they," she stopped as she locked eyes with Luke in the mirror. Her phone slipped down from her grip and she turned to face both twins, horror spreading over their sweet faces.

Screw Harry Vogel. She'd let the officials deal with him. Unlatching her seat belt she maneuvered out of her spot and wedged herself on the console, facing them both as their faces cracked into hysterics.

"Shhh, no, no, no, no. Boys, it's okay. It's okay!" A hard lump formed in her own throat and she took a deep breath, knowing full well that if she cried, then it was all over. "Your parents did not crash. They are totally fine. I'm so sorry I even said that. I was angry with my friend, Harry. That's all. I promise."

Nick choked out a final sob and a smile emerged on his wet mouth. "They're okay?" he squeaked as Luke let out a sniffle. Bo offered a broad smile in return and cupped each boy's cheek in her two hands.

"They are safe. They're okay. They just needed a little time alone, that's all."

Satisfied with her answer, the boys returned to an innocent game of I Spy, allowing Bo to resume her place behind the wheel before shooting off a group text to the family, including her brothers and her sisters' boyfriends this time.

Talked to the owner of the plane. His name is Harrison Vogel. Says plane was in operating condition, but the radio is dead. Call airport authority NOW and 911.

As she hit SEND, a text appeared from Harry.

One more thing. So sorry, Bo. I'll tell the FAA... I was doing work on the plane recently and had to make some replacements. Right now the plane has no beacon.

Chapter 22: Ben

He pulled Erica closer to him, tucking her slight body behind his after a moment assessing the situation. Black bears were no joke.

Ben only knew because he had definitely seen lots of black bears in his life. The sight was startling, enough to snap him out of his grief entirely. This is what survival mode felt like.

Erica forced herself up under his arm, refusing his protection in favor of watching.

He muttered, "I know I put the cap back on the Gatorade. I can't imagine..." his voice trailed off as they hushed in time for the bear to smarten up, haul its weight onto the nose of the plane, and reach a furry arm inside the cockpit.

Erica gasped, and Ben glanced down at her before returning his attention to the plane. Empty-handed, it was unsatisfied but determined and hefted itself through the open windshield. Ben wished he had a camera. The sight of a massive black bear crawling through a busted-out plane window was equal parts horrifying and hilarious. But in the pit of his stomach, he knew it was really bad news. He should have kept the Gatorade on his body, rather than leave it behind for even five minutes. The sugary drink was sure to attract any number of scavengers, and especially bears.

If mountain-born folks knew one thing, it was that outside food meant bears, especially at dusk and dawn. It was the very reason Ben was in charge of pulling the trash into the barn night after night. It was the reason he got a butt whooping the one time he didn't and a bear ate its way through their trash can.

"Oh no, I'm so sorry," his wife whispered below him.

He'd have asked her to explain, but the bear did it for them, hauling from the back compartment her handbag and propping it on the plane in order to dig its beefy claws through the leather, shredding the strap and withdrawing a half-eaten pack of Red Vines, which it promptly swept into its eager bear mouth.

Erica and her damned licorice. But it wasn't that she had left open food that bothered him the most.

He bent his face down to her ear, whispering fiercely, "You had *food* this *whole time!?*"

She looked up at him, batting her dark lashes as she answered, "I was *rationing*."

Chapter 23: Erica

She was going to share the stupid Red Vines. No question. But since Ben was rationing his Gatorade, well, she followed her husband's lead, petty though it may be.

He muttered a curse under his breath, though she was pretty sure she detected a hint of smile, too. Even now, she realized, as they watched a massive bear thrash about the wreckage, scratching the metal of the plane and digging beneath it as if to find more food, the scene was comical. But fear pricked at her spine when the beast seemed to give up on his search and stood on his hind legs, growling into the air, his gaping bear mouth sending echoes through the trees.

Ben grabbed her waist and deftly twirled her behind the tree.

Facing her, he held a hand to his mouth before gesticulating what he thought was happening, but she already knew.

The monster was calling his friends and family to join in the apparent feast of the fallen flying machine.

Ever so slowly, they each craned their neck around to confirm: two more bears peeked out from the far side of the woods before ambling gleefully to the plane.

Ben shook his head, and then motioned her closer to him. Again, he grabbed her around the waist, his movements swift and smooth, so that her back was against the tree and he was facing the plane. His body pinning hers in place, she couldn't help but notice how sensual the moment was. They hadn't slept together... in bed or elsewhere... in eons, it felt like. She couldn't remember the last time she really and truly *felt* like it. Right now, despite everything (or perhaps because of it), she *felt* like it. Ben's hips pressed into hers thanks to the height allotted to her by the forest floor and a thick root. His capable hands cupped her waist as he leaned into her to steady himself as he poked his head around the thick width of the tree.

Erica felt herself warm from within and her expression moved from fear, to humor, to... something soft. She moved one hand from his shoulder down his chest, and he flashed a look at her.

Erica knew her husband well. And he knew her. She saw recognition in his gaze even as he took her hand from his chest and peeled it off. Heart sinking, she moved her other hand from his shoulder and crossed both arms over her chest, her nostrils flaring and eyes narrowing up at him.

Ben ignored the miniature tantrum and leaned down to whisper again into her ear, his voice like a snake's. "You're trying to come on to me in the middle of the woods, after asking for a divorce, after a plane crash, on the way to my dad's... *funeral* potentially, while a family of *bears* digs through our *shelter*?" He leaned back, cocking his head around the tree after spitting out a succinct summary of events.

Erica wasn't sure if she ought to laugh or cry. Or just pull Ben closer and hug the hate out of him. Out of herself.

She didn't, instead mumble-whispering a teenaged "So-rry."

He directed his attention back to her and weighed their next course of action. After a few beats, he bent again, his voice still quiet but deeper now, "We'll talk about it later. We have to stay here until they give us space."

Erica nodded her head, averting her eyes as she felt heat of embarrassment wave through her like a tide. She was an idiot. On several counts. And now, she had time to do nothing except think about that. Her idiocy in taking that stupid therapist's advice. Her idiocy in agreeing to join Ben on this trip.

Actually, her idiocy actually began when she decided out of the blue that, despite having everything she ever could have wanted, in fact, she wanted even more. A daughter.

Why couldn't she settle for a Golden Retriever? She and Ben both loved animals. The boys would have been thrilled. But no, she had to go all out.

And then, after thinking *that*, guilt punched her in the gut. How could she regret wanting a daughter? Did that mean she regretted carrying her little daughter, even if for a brief few weeks? A hard lump grew in her throat and panic washed over her. She'd have to swallow her sobs. The seriousness of the situation coalesced before her and she regained her game face, pushing away bad thoughts about the past. Pushing away bad thoughts about her choices. Pushing away bad thoughts about Ben, who didn't know when to be soft or hard. And as she pushed away all those bad thoughts, one thought clouded back into her head and her body.

Longing for her husband.

Chapter 24: Bo

Arriving in Maplewood felt surreal. Bo hadn't been back to town in a couple months, but it felt like much longer. As pine trees converged upon the SUV, little reminders of her childhood pushed their way up, grounding her and unsettling her all at once.

Camping trips with Ben and Erica when they were just teenagers. Going to the movies once or twice in the summer, when they scrounged enough extra cash to cover tickets and a kid-sized bag of over-salted popcorn. Farm chores. Ranch work.

The boys snoozed in the back seat, having succumbed to their exhaustion only once they had passed through the canyon and were careening around the bends of the reservation.

Now, coasting into town, she ticked off the chain stores and restaurants that had reared their ugly heads into the rapidly expanding small town. Hank's Hardware and Small Engine Repair would soon be replaced by House Central. Leslie Zick's bakery by Donuts R Us. Big Ed's Country Market by ABCO Wholesaler. She shook her head, wondering if there was ever an escape from big, fat jerks.

Finally, after Bo crested the hill up the highway, she turned right down Ingleheart Lane, the dirt road which led directly and only to her family's age-old log cabin, which sat on a sprawling fifty acres, abutting exclusively to the national forest.

She'd taken for granted just how nice a spot her family owned, even if the ranch and farm were out of commission. Anyway, her brothers' orchard and event space (*the BARn*) was thriving. No need to grow your own food when you could pay cash for equally fresh fare at the local market, or at least, that was the motto Margaret and Dick Delaney finally adopted once their slave children were grown and gone. Still, Bo was proud of Robbie and Alan for taking up her parents' legacy and making something of the family land.

She threw the Caddy into park and shut the engine, peering over her shoulder at the boys and deciding she had to wake them. Just as she pushed open the heavy SUV door, Anna stepped out the front door. Behind her marched Mary and their mother, Margaret. Even from yards away, Bo took note of Mary's and Anna's tear-streaked faces.

For the first time, Bo felt a pain in her heart that she'd been squashing down. Her mom walked up to her and wrapped her in a bear hug, which had the effect of unleashing a torrential downpour for all four women.

After mopping her face with her tee-shirt, Bo looked past her mom. "Where are Robbie and Alan and Dad?"

Anna answered, her voice fragile. "Dad is at the airport with Kurt. The others joined the police to set up the search base. The FAA has some people at the airport conducting interviews. Bo, you have to go there now. They're waiting for you."

Bo glanced through her open car door to the boys, sleeping peacefully like a set of mirror images. She swallowed a sob and looked back to her sisters and mother. "I had no idea it was this serious. I mean, maybe they just took a side trip or something?" Her voice pleading, guilt pooling in her stomach.

"Phoenix, Tucson, Flagstaff, Albuquerque, Vegas... nothing, Roberta," her mother's voice rose into a crescendo of blame. "Whose plane were they in?"

Bo darted her eyes to Anna and Mary, looking for back-up. When their eyebrows lifted in question, Bo scrubbed her hands across her face, sniffling in and coughing out before launching into an impromptu explanation.

"Harrison Vogel. My writing professor. Teacher. Writing teacher from Tucson Community. I've been taking a class, trying to build my skill set," she winced at the stupid excuse before continuing. "He was tutoring me. We... we're... we *were* close." She glanced up, measuring their reactions. Anna took a step forward.

"Are you dating this guy?"

Bo replied, lamely, "Not anymore. Maybe I never was. But he's not a bad guy. Just... and the plane, I just spoke with him and like I texted you... the plane was fine other than the radio and beacon. Everything else should have been working. No reason for it to go down."

Anger clouded Mary's face. "Where the hell is he, Bo? Is he even worried about his plane?"

Shock crossed the other three women's faces. Mary never cursed.

Bo opened her mouth to reply, but her mother cut a hand up through the air, silencing the girls. "We know he's not *worried*, Mary. He's on the lam for goodness sakes. Roberta, the FAA are trying to track him down. He's not responding to phone calls. Officers are en route to his home and are following your lead on his conference. We'll take the boys inside," she strode past Bo and opened the back car door. "You need to go directly to the airport. Anna will join you. Mary and I are staying here and monitoring the phone lines and email, in case Erica or Ben reach out."

Speechless, Bo simply nodded and pulled herself back up into the driver's seat. She desperately needed to pee, and she was dying of thirst, but she followed orders and set off to Maplewood's windy, dusty airport. Silence filled the vehicle as the sisters stewed over what may be.

"UNACCEPTABLE." DICK Delaney and Kurt Cutler stood, backs facing Anna and Bo as they approached the kiosk where their father talked with three official-looking men as a handful of others who framed the desk. Bo's father's booming voice echoed across the tiled floor and swirled around the baggage carousel stalling nearby.

Bo flicked a glance to Anna, whose focus was trained ahead. Kurt saw them first, twisting around at the women's approach. He nodded severely before stepping aside to let the sisters join the meeting.

"I'm Bo," she announced sheepishly as she held a hand out to the tallest man. Anna offered her palm and they swiftly made introductions before the portly officer swept Bo into the windowed room that stood behind the kiosk. Nervously, she glanced back at her dad and Anna, who picked up on the hint.

"I'll come, too," Anna said as she stepped up to the open doorway.

The officer waved her in and pointed to a corner chair. At first, Bo worried that her lurid tale of an affair with a teacher would be awkward and painful and most of all useless. But it wasn't. Freedom swept through her, and she laid out all the facts, even taking care to emphasize that while Harry had assured her the plane was fine, she actually had her doubts. It may have been in poor working order. And, if they hadn't found out yet, there was no beacon.

Chapter 25: Ben

It wasn't his first encounter with a bear. The Stevens farm was a hot spot for these damn things. But, it was his first encounter with a bear, out in the open, with no house or barn to hide in. No weapons. Nothing.

As they hid behind the tree just yards away from the three beasts, Ben considered his priorities and his course of action.

1. He had to protect Erica. No matter how bad things were between them, she was a woman. Still *his* woman. The mother of his children. She came first. Always had. Always would, even if they did… well, even if things did end. Which, maybe they wouldn't.
2. Wait out the bears. Regardless of if they were staying with the plane or hiking toward town, they couldn't move until they were in the clear. Couldn't risk an attack. It would be fatal, no doubt. Even a scratch on the arm could be fatal in the woods- no medic, no running water, no way to tell if the bears were rabid, though he doubted it. No first aid kit.

Wait a minute. The plane very well should have a first aid kit. Ben would have to check.

Despite his fitness, holding himself against the tree was beginning to cramp him. Ben glanced at the ground to assess the underbrush, of which there was little. He then looked at Erica, locking eyes. She hadn't worn much makeup that morning, which he liked. Her clear eyes wet and waiting, her mouth still, she bore an expression he couldn't quite read. It wasn't worry, really. Or fear.

Hope?

Love…?

He pressed his lips together in an attempt at a smile and was met with batting eyelashes and a devilish grin and then a giggle emerged from her soft, pink lips.

Stop it. He wanted to say.

You wanted a divorce! He'd like to shout.

We are moments away from a bear attack! He just might scream.

Instead, he gripped her face in his hands, his fingers laced around her ears and up into her blonde hair, and then bent close by the side of her head, controlled rage seething out from between his teeth.

To one of the bears, it might look like they were kissing. But he wasn't.

Whispering closely to her ear, he shushed her and then explained that they needed to change positions. She simply nodded in return. He cocked his head around to see all three bears were now out of the plane and digging into his duffle bag. He frowned, praying that they'd leave it behind.

Slowly, he motioned to her to join him on the forest floor, where he eased himself down with his arms until his lean, athletic body lay perfectly still beneath scant saplings. Erica, a hand over her mouth, cautiously joined him. He could imagine the rocks and sticks poking up into the bare skin of her legs and arms, but she kept it together. No stupid nervous giggles. No complaining.

She was like a cat. He swallowed hard, looking away from her pretty face and back to the bears.

They lay together like that for what felt like another hour (Ben kicked himself for forgetting his watch that morning), as the bears did another check of the cabin and the two now-shredded bags before tumbling away back into the woods.

Once they'd disappeared for what had to be at least ten minutes, Ben held a hand out to keep Erica in place and quiet as he pushed up and prowled toward the plane. He walked its length and circled it before doubling back to the woods opposite where they had lain. Slowly and silently, he walked into the woods several yards, scoping through the trees as far as he could see.

It was clear. For now.

Before returning to Erica, he stopped at the plane, picking up his shredded duffle and stepping back behind a wing and out of sight from his wife. His breath catching in his throat, he slowly stuck a hand into the limp fabric that remained, reaching into its deepest corner.

Thank God.
It was still there.

He looked up and over the wing to see Erica watching him. He wanted to open the little case to see it, check on it. But he couldn't start that convo now. It wasn't time. They needed to set their plan and execute it. Waste no time on feelings or anything else. He had to get home to his dad first.

With less caution, he walked back to get Erica, pulling her to her feet. She brushed twigs and soil from her front side, and Ben glanced away, feeling too awkward to watch as her hands frisked her chest and flat stomach and bare thighs. A pit formed in his stomach as he thought back to the divorce. The pit grew deeper as the thought of his dad replaced the divorce threat. He was desperate to know of the old man's condition. Was he already dead? Was he alive but unconscious? If he was conscious, did he know that his son was missing? It sure wouldn't help his condition. He snapped out of it, remembering to focus.

"We can't stay now," he pointed out as he followed Erica over to the plane where she grabbed her purse to see what was left of it and in it.

She glared at him over her shoulder, still not speaking.

He raised his voice only slightly across the small clearing. "Erica, black bears now see this location like Nicky and Luke see your purse. It's snack central. It doesn't matter if they ate *all* your licorice or drank *all* our Gatorade. They've marked this place. They'll be back. There's no question. You know that just as well as I do."

She spread her hands through the slobbered leather, popping out a lipstick, some random papers, her cell, and bag of wet wipes. The rest of what had been in there was now scattered about the forest floor, unceremoniously. Erica bent down to comb through contents, finding nothing of value, apparently, because she rose and clapped her hands upon her shorts before crossing them over her chest.

"So? What do we do, then?" she asked, her mouth set in a line, her eyes impassive.

He mirrored her body language and expression, crossing his arms and allowing his face to fall flat before launching into his game. "We decide what, if anything, we take, and we head due north," he paused to gesture behind himself before continuing. "If we don't reach the highway by dusk, we set up camp as best as we can, then keep walking tomorrow morning."

"So you have no idea how far we are from the highway?" she asked.

"I know we are no more than about forty miles. Probably no less than thirty."

He could read her face as she prepared the math in her head before working it out aloud. "If we walk slowly, say 20 minutes per mile on average, that comes out to about 800 minutes. Divided by sixty..." she stalled, bending down to grab a twig, clear a square of earth, and write out a division problem in the soil. "Eight hundred divided by... sixty," she murmured as she drew. "One, two hundred, carry the three... Okay, so like 13 hours on foot," she finished. "*If* you're right about our location in relation to Maplewood Highway. And *if* we don't veer off course."

"I think forty is a conservative estimate," he replied.

She considered it for a minute, glancing around the clearing and into the woods, as if she felt the bears staring in at them. "Okay. Let's do it," she answered at last, allowing a defeated smile in his direction. "What are we taking? Got any matches? Your sunglasses, maybe?" He'd moved to the cockpit, by then, to dig around for a compass, map, anything that might help. He felt Erica pass behind him and he swiveled around in time to see her pick up his duffle.

"Drop it." His voice was entirely humorless through gritted teeth as his body went rigid. She let the bag fall to the ground and looked up at him, confusion filling her face.

He swallowed hard, preparing to explain himself. It could, after all, change everything.

But he decided not to. The plan had to come first. Survival before feelings. Survival came first.

Chapter 26: Erica

What was in the bag? And how did it withstand a virtual bear attack? Erica dropped it to the ground, waiting for an explanation. None came, of course. She moved away as he continued rummaging in the cockpit. Feeling the extent of her exhaustion and thirst and hunger, found a felled log and sank down onto it as she eyed him through the empty window.

Evidence of an affair. It had to be. Maybe a handwritten note from some Southwestern fan. Years of marriage to a college football coach had taught her one thing: Ben was *wanted*.

A note, though? It wasn't 1950. And his phone was safely dead.

Condoms. That would give him away. The thought made her want to vomit. Her pulse quickened and she held a hand to her mouth, stilling the gag reflex. Hatred swelled in her heart as she stared at the man she used to know.

She was right to ask for the divorce.

Old Ben would never even so much as glance at a pretty woman. What changed? She racked her brain thinking of all the other signs. There were many...

No sleeping together (she ignored the fact that it was a mutual decision).
No date nights.
No talking.
And mostly...
No sex.

She would blame herself if she weren't so damn mad about... what *was* she mad at about? The miscarriage, obviously. But, was there more than that? Had she really allowed the miscarriage to push her this far?

Well, if he was cheating, then it didn't matter, anyway. They were *so* done. *So* done.

Ben descended from the plane, doubling back behind the wing to grab his bag and stick an arm inside. His back faced her, and she wanted to sprint over and rip it out of his hand, holding whatever it was up in the air so she could yell, *See!? See? You ARE awful! You're the bad one! You ruined everything!*

She even stood, heart racing, and took a few steps through pine needles and scratchy saplings, tiny pebbles and twigs tickling the soles of her feet as they wedged themselves into her sandals. She could feel everything and nothing all at once. Her skin itched and warmed in the emerging sun as she crept forward.

"What is it, Ben?" Calmly, she braced herself against the plane before she realized he was shaking. His entire body. His head had fallen forward onto his chest, his hands clasped in front of him, maybe even holding the awful evidence, regretting everything awful he had ever done to her or not done to her.

Suddenly, he whipped around, facing her now and holding a small, velvet case.

"Here," he cried out, thrusting the case at her. "I can't take it anymore, Erica. Here," after pushing into her hand, he crumpled back against the wing of the plane, wiping his eyes and sniffling for a moment.

Frowning, she looked down at the purple fabric, soft in her hands. "What is this?" she asked, her voice low, gentle.

"I ordered it a few weeks ago. I," he faltered before finding his footing, a final sniffle escaping as he collected himself. "Erica, I could never talk about it. But I was just as sad as you. Some days even sadder. It arrived at the post office two days ago. I wasn't sure if I was going to have the balls to give it to you after all, especially after you asked for a divorce. But, well, there you are. I'm sorry, Erica."

Tears welling in her eyes she slowly cracked open the box to reveal a pendant. She pulled it up to her face, studying it carefully.

The figure of an angel and inscribed along the wings:

Baby Girl Stevens, forever in our hearts

"*I can't breathe,*" she whispered to herself, emotion washing through her, unstoppable. Lightheaded, she braced herself against the wing and melted down onto the cool earth, clutching the pendant to her heart. Sobs heaved through her like earthquakes. All over again, her heart broke into millions of pieces.

But this time, as Ben knelt down beside her, pulling her into his lap and stroking her hair, she felt like it might actually start to heal.

Chapter 27: Bo

After nearly an hour of questions, the officer directed Bo to stay at the airport and continue to try and reach Harry. He passed her cell phone back to her once he'd documented the recent texts. He trusted that she wasn't part of some elaborate kidnapping scene and denied her offer to trace her info. Then again, she probably didn't need to give permission for that. They could very well get a full record of texts and phone calls without her cooperation at all.

Bo and Anna both cringed when he used that word: *case*. It was a reminder that things were looking bad. It was a reminder that Bo screwed up.

As always.

Bo was born to be bad. That's what her brothers joked when she hit junior high and had her first official run in with local law enforcement (she ripped off the tail of a rival school's mascot during a football game). Anna had thought it was exciting. Their parents were livid. Dick Delaney wasn't quick to temper, but the rage he and Margaret had unleashed on Bo was unparalleled. It even set her straight, for a while.

Until high school hit, and with that… boys. Bo's dark beauty stood out amongst the blonde brigade that made up the cheerleading squad and student council. Boys were drawn to her inky hair and brilliantly light eyes. And she was drawn to them, earning her first boyfriend, Billy Flanagan, in a fist fight her sophomore year. Billy, a bad boy himself, made Bo his own and together they caused trouble for teachers and other students on an ongoing basis.

The Delaneys were very much relieved when their oldest and most disappointing daughter graduated (miraculously) from high school and made her way from Arizona town to Arizona town, stopping only for boys and booze, until she finally found her way to college, hammering out a degree and running up a student loan that was worth more than her life.

Writing was a given for Bo. She'd always enjoyed spinning stories so detailed in their complications that her lies were lost in the mess.

But creative writing didn't quite pan out. She'd finally landed a few gigs in Tucson and fell in love with its eclectic southwestern charm well enough to commit to living there.

Meeting and falling in with her post-grad adult ed. teacher, sadly, felt like a serious upgrade. She had visions of bringing Harry home to Maplewood to show off to her family. *Look ma! Bo can land someone decent and educated and good.*

Now, as she followed Anna and the officer out of the little office space, she stifled a bitter laugh.

Once again, Roberta Delaney had done something bad.

She joined Anna behind the kiosk as the men discussed the next steps. The family members were taken aback by the drastic measures. They were both comforting and worrying. Air Force was called to cover the skies above and around the flight path. They were solid, and they were the best bet of spotting disrupted topiary, the downed plane, or—maybe—smoke.

Meanwhile, they'd extend the ground search statewide, then regionally, pulling in support from New Mexico, Colorado, and Nevada at minimum. California after that. As they spoke, three, large-scale ground rescue search operations were forming in Tucson, Globe, and Maplewood.

"Why the Air Force, though?" Bo interjected, her eyebrows pinched in fear.

"Standard procedure ma'am," the taller officer responded, smiling sadly. "Their resources are bar none, and we take advantage of their help even in lesser incidents."

Everything he said was meant to reassure her, but none of it did.

Anna, Dick, and Kurt were nodding along as Ben's mom and brother walked in, accompanied by another nameless security guard. Brief introductions were made and the short officer brought them up to speed as Ben's mom sobbed quietly into her son's shoulder.

Finally, the officer concluded the plan with, "It'll be a help to make a press release. If anyone heard anything, we may be able to motivate them to reach out, assuming their information results in the discovery of your daughter and her husband."

Bo's dad rubbed a hand along his jaw. "We'll do whatever it takes. We don't have much, but we'll put up our savings, and, ah..." his voice cracked and he dipped his head down to his hands. Anna wrapped her arms around the weeping man and joined in silent crying.

Kurt stepped toward the officer, lowering his voice. Bo kept an eye on him, fear and worry coursing through her veins. She didn't know Mary's fiancé very well. But she knew what he could offer.

"We can put up the reward." he responded for Dick. "Money is no issue. Let's get this moving."

Bo flashed a glance to their father who offered a hand to Kurt. But Kurt pulled the older man into a close hug, wrapping Anna, too.

Tears pricking down Bo's cheeks, a sob escaped her mouth and she fell into the group embrace. As she held on to Anna's back, an arm wrapped itself around her shoulders, the hand squeezing her tightly.

It was her dad. And even in the face of everything bad, it gave her hope. And even more than that, it gave her resolve. Resolve to never again make a bad choice. She swallowed the lump in her throat and dried her tears on the back of Anna's shirt, pressing her face firmly into the smell of her sister. Her family. Her world.

The officials gave the family a moment before one cleared his voice. "Time is of the essence. Every moment counts," one of them broke in.

Dick Delaney pushed back from his daughters and future son-in-law, his face dry but grim. He replied evenly, "What do *you* think happened, officer?" Bo noticed Ben's mom pat her face and crane her neck for the reply.

Each of the uniforms solemnly shook his head before the taller one cleared his voice to respond. "It could be he swept her away on a surprise vacation. It could be they fell off the flight path and lost their way well into New Mexico or farther north. Could be they ran out of fuel and floated down. Could be . . ."

"A crash," Bo finished for him.

Chapter 28: Ben

They held each other for a long while as Erica calmed down and each one emerged from the embrace with dry faces and careful smiles.

"I take it back, Ben," she whispered as she looked up into his eyes.

He held her chin in place with his thumb and forefinger. "Take what back? Your vows? Because you kind of already did that." It was meant as a joke, but even he heard the harshness behind the words.

She answered, "I know. I'm so sorry Ben." She bit down on her lip, lifting her brows up to him. "I was selfish. I was . . . dwelling. And I couldn't understand how you could move on so easily. But," she paused, looking to him for permission to continue. When he nodded, she went on. "But, I take it back, if I can. I take it back so much. I know that I never *wanted* divorce. I never did."

Ben was learning not to brush things off. They had to deal with it. Here and now, bears be damned. Rescue be damned. Everything be damned for the time being. "Then why did you ask for one?"

She blinked and crinkled her brows, looking down at the pendant still pressed into her palm, its chain now safely strung around her neck. "Something had to change in our marriage, Ben." With caution, she peeked up at his reaction.

But, the thing of it was... he agreed. Things had gotten bad. The necklace wasn't even meant to resolve their issues. He needed closure for himself, too. That was truth of the matter. His relationship with Erica was so far gone that he hadn't even looked at it as a means to a truce.

But here they were, coming damn close to a ceasefire.

"How come you didn't, I don't know...why not a separation? Or... why didn't you give me any warning?"

Her answer was swift. "Ben, we don't talk anymore. I had no opportunity for it. We got to be so... disconnected. All the little things became one big thing that by the time I was ready to move past the miscarriage, I realized that I also had moved past our marriage. I hate to say that, but it's the truth. A divorce seemed logical. No longer would I lie in bed praying that you'd creep into my room when you came home from practice. Or wake up and go into the kitchen to find a sweet note. My disappointment in you became all-consuming. I'm sorry."

Ouch. That hurt. He knew Erica was a smart woman. And he knew she was hurt. But how could divorce be logical? The boys... their life together... all a series of logical choices? He didn't buy it. And as for disappointment? That was life. Was she really this fragile?

"Seemed like an emotional decision, Erica." His voice was firm but gentle.

To his surprise, she agreed immediately. "You're right. It wasn't logic. It was emotion. I suppose I felt that for so long it was coming. You care so much about your career, and I love your passion for it, I do, Ben. But we get the leftovers. Luke and Nicky hardly know you. They don't understand why we had to move away from their school and their friends. I guess I thought that if we detached ourselves from you, they wouldn't feel like your absence was a result of your prioritizing football, but instead a result of their parents' fighting. Sounds awful now that I say that. I know." She dropped her head down to her chest, her body folding in in what could only be described as shame.

But there was no shame.

She was right.

Football was his world, and his home had become a landing place, little more. "I'm so sorry. I'm just so sorry."

She leaned into him and he pulled her closer, kissing the top of her head before she took him by surprise, pulling herself up and straddling him.

He looked at her, question in his eyes.

She answered with a smile before saying, "Ben Stevens, maybe we can work on it. Maybe it's not too late? Maybe this is—" She flailed her hands around, reminding him of their ridiculous circumstances "—our chance?" His mind floated uncontrollably to his father and then his two sons. His daughter in heaven. His wife on his lap.

"Erica, we have no choice. You are stranded with me, after all." And with that, Ben pulled her face in to his, a flashback to their summer camping trips sufficiently suffocating his current fears and worries as his lips met his wife's, and he realized just how perfect she still was.

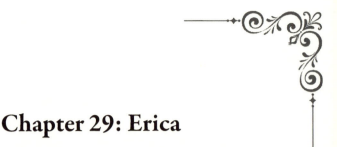

Chapter 29: Erica

She felt like a new woman. Different. Higher. Better. She felt whole again.

Agreeing heartily, now, that they could and should start walking, she wove her fingers through Ben's and they took off, due north, toward Maplewood Highway. Their bags were shredded to the point of being useless, and so Ben stashed the bare essentials in his pockets: his wallet, packed with cash Erica had in hers; Chapstick; both their phones; and the mini pack of wet wipes. Erica's job was to carry the leftover plastic of one of the Gatorade bottles, since it was intact enough to use as a drinking vessel. They were both surprised he didn't have an entire extra outfit or his first aid kit. He said he kept those items in his locker and only brought the duffle that day to hide the necklace. The fact that the plane had no first aid kit came as no surprise.

Hand in hand they walked, Ben leading her through brambles and saplings, over felled logs, and through a maze of thick forest flora. They walked in silence, keeping a steady pace, though they were uncertain how far they'd gone. Once they'd been walking for some time, Erica wondered aloud, "Should we have laid a trail of breadcrumbs? What if we are veering off course?"

"I'm keeping track of the sun and eyeing the compass," he called behind him, throwing her a crooked grin. Her heart sank as she recognized the twins in his expression.

She was doing everything in her power to be strong enough to set aside her worry over them, but now that she and Ben were on better terms, she needed his comfort. "Do you think the boys are okay?"

Ben turned his body and walked backward for a few strides, answering her steadily, "Bo has crappy taste in men. But I trust her with the boys. I'm sure she's distracting them with wild stories and games. Bo's fun, remember." He turned back before adding, "It's my dad I'm worried about."

She couldn't read him, but she pressed the issue, because she was worried too. "Do you know what happened? Exactly?"

Ben's jaw tensed before he blew out a sigh and answered her. "It wasn't looking good. Last I heard he was in the ICU, out cold."

Erica tugged on his hand, pulling him to a stop.

"What?" he asked, frowning.

"Your dad is one of the strongest men I know. He's gonna be fine Ben. And we're gonna get there in time to know that for sure." She offered a weak smile, but he just shook his head.

"I hope."

And again, for another long while, they walked in silence, traversing the same terrain over and again with little to entertain them.

HOURS HAD PASSED, UNDOUBTEDLY. The sun had completed a half circle above them, and Erica's mouth had grown dry and chalky. Her empty stomach flipped and growled, and the cuts on her arms and legs began to itch. Her legs were beginning to tire beneath her, and her lower back ached. But she kept mum about it all, following Ben's silent lead. Though now, she was sick of replaying the boys' scared faces in her head. Ben's dad's lifeless body, pale and prone on a hospital bed. She was sick of wondering when they'd see something, anything. Even a piece of litter would be a welcome sight by now.

"Let's play twenty questions. You know, pass the time." But just as Ben turned to respond, the lip of Erica's sandal caught on a root, sending her flying forward.

She felt like she was in slow motion, drifting through the air past an unprepared Ben, arms flailing ineffectively as she landed, her head missing the fat trunk of an oak tree by mere inches.

Once she was down on the ground, her nose mushed against dry pine needles, arms doing little to catch the fall, she let out a laugh. Ben had caught the back of her second shirt as she fell, stretching it against her chest, preventing her from hitting her head on the tree.

But for some reason a dreamlike quality coated the experience, and Erica didn't hear Ben join in her laughter as he lifted her up from the forest floor.

She steadied herself against him, her eyes narrowing on his delicious lips and puppy dog gaze and sharp jawline and she realized she felt drunk and then Ben began to speak and she noticed both his hands were supporting her weight and just before everything went dark she heard him as he whispered and his voice was a million miles away and she could have sworn she heard, "*Erica, you're bleeding.*"

Chapter 30: Bo

Bo hated being stuck at the airport. She wanted to be canvassing the woods with her brothers and dad and Kurt and Anna's boyfriend, Dutch, and a whole swarm of strangers.

But instead, she sat there in a private room near the security offices, the plastic chair beneath her growing slick with sweat from her thighs. She didn't even know why she was still there.

Anna returned from the bathroom and plopped into the chair next to her.

"No word," Bo sighed out, knowing what Anna's first question would be.

Anna frowned and leaned forward, her elbows on her knees as she pried for more info. *Who was Harry? What did he look like? Had Bo ever been on the plane? Did they at least check it out before they took off?*

The last question sparked hope in her chest.

"Yes. Ben did a quick walk-around and checked the control panel or whatever before they left. He didn't say anything."

Anna had no reply.

"Anna, he was so anxious to get up here. He couldn't wait. I don't know, maybe something was wrong with the plane. And if so, it was definitely my fault," Bo whined.

Her sister pressed a hand to Bo's shoulder. "No. It's not your fault. You were trying to help. And anyways, who's to say they crashed? Or, if they did crash, who's to say it was because of the plane? There are a million reasons planes crash, trust me."

Bo threw a glance to her. "Like what? And how do you know?"

"Remember Jake?"

Bo rolled her eyes. One of Anna's many conquests. Of course she remembered Jake. He was... filthy rich, for starters... but he was also weird. Like a hot Howard Hughes. "Yeah?"

"He owned a private airport in California, remember? He told me all these wild stories about how small planes get into trouble. Pilots drunk or high. Altitude sickness. Losing control happens easier than you'd think. Plus other forces. Weather, for one."

Bo interrupted, "Obviously it isn't the weather."

"I know that. I'm just saying that flying in a small plane is extraordinarily dangerous."

Biting her lip and slumping over onto her knees, she took that to heart. She knew it was dangerous. Harry had mentioned it over and again. And yet, she allowed her sister to board a flight with an upset amateur pilot in a plane about which Bo knew nothing.

She officially sucked at making good decisions, for herself *and* for others.

"Hey, ladies," the hint of a southern drawl cut into her self-loathing, and she and Anna looked up to see a new man join them. His steel-toed boots cut into her line of sight. She followed his long legs up to a surprisingly familiar face.

Bo's eyes flashed. She'd recognize him anywhere.

"Keegan?" Bo asked, glancing to Anna to see if she noticed. It was one of the Flanagan boys. The oldest, in fact. All grown up.

He nodded gravely.

Bo stood and took a step up to him. "What are you doing here?" She was confused.

He held up a badge in reply. "Deputy Sheriff with Apache County, Northeastern Arizona Rescue Association. Assigned to this and any other missing persons case." He cleared his throat, letting the weight of his words settle on the Delaney sisters.

His cool demeanor instantly transported Bo back to high school, when she first met Keegan. He was Billy's older brother and a full two grades ahead of them. He'd always been elusive and shy. Brooding, even. But he'd also always been hot as hellfire.

Now, however, the fact that he was *still* hot wasn't at the forefront of her concerns. However, their close connection did give her renewed hope. Not that the FAA or feds or military weren't enough to help find Erica. It's just that *knowing* one of the assigned local officers was a comfort. That was one good thing about small towns. Even assholes took care of other assholes… if they were from the same dinky place. And if the Flanagan brothers were assholes, Bo was one, too.

"Do you know anything, yet? Do you have a sense of what might have happened, Keegan? We feel helpless." Bo ran her hands over her face and up through her hair as she pressed her back into the wall and then swallowed hard before training her eyes on him. He looked exactly the same but fifteen years older. His thick head of hair and bright green eyes underscored his Irish genes. Full lips stood out from a once-freckled face. He'd grown out of the freckles, and all that was left was a hardened expression, not unlike his little brother's resting jerk face... the same one teenaged Bo used to swoon over. A pit formed in her stomach as she wondered just what Keegan would think of her now, practically implicated in her sister's disappearance.

As if reading her mind, he swooped in with a reassuring response. "It's not your fault, Roberta." She winced at the use of her given name. It sounded awkward and formal.

"Bo," she corrected.

Indifference crossed his face as he ignored it and went on, looking from sister to sister. "Actually, though, yes, we do have some news." He glanced down at a leather-bound notebook, giving Bo enough time to inspect his ensemble. She'd never have predicted that a Flanagan boy would turn professional. Then again, she hadn't kept track. For all she knew, they could be billionaire CEOs. Not Keegan, though. His look was tailored but casual. Neat but subdued. A black button-down, Wranglers, and steel-toed boots. He turned a page before continuing. "Harrison Vogel, your, eh, boyfriend?" He lifted his gaze to meet Bo's, and she bit a lip, darting her eyes anywhere but into Keegan's.

"Ex," she muttered.

"We got in touch with him. He is out of town. At a conference in California for work. Anyway, he came clean, explaining that the radio had been malfunctioning and he'd removed the beacon for maintenance. He swore up and down that nothing else was out-of-order. Unfortunately, the FAA guys don't buy it. If it were just the radio, fine. But for both crucial instruments to be out-of-order means that he hadn't kept the craft in good working order."

She desperately wanted to ask if he was in trouble. She wanted him locked up for good. Shame on him. He could have easily denied them use of his plane, explaining that it was a piece of crap. But he *let* other people board. What a total and utter loser. A bad guy, even. But Bo had to admit to herself that she'd heard it in his voice. The hesitation. Something was off, and she chalked it up to fear of commitment. In fact, Harry was both afraid of commitment *and* afraid of responsibility. She shook her head and frowned. "You think the plane failed? Like, died or something? Mid-flight?"

Keegan blinked and dropped his hands to his sides. "Maybe, yeah. It's clear that Vogel is shady, and the FAA is following up. He'll face some fines, at minimum. But right now, of course, the focus is on the recovery mission."

Chapter 31: Ben

He was freaking out. But there was no time for it. As Erica fell, he'd clung to her shirt, preventing her from landing headlong into a massive oak trunk. But that would have been safer than what actually resulted.

As she'd twisted around, her face grew white within moments. The red liquid seeping down her leg had torn his attention from her oddly goofy smile. Initially, he thought she'd started her period. But there was so much blood, pooling and pouring past her knee, down her shin, darkening the leather of her sandals. He grabbed both her hands to steady her and get a closer look, but her body grew heavy and he had to reposition his hands under her arms until she passed right out.

Frantic and confused, he caught her as she slipped down, and carried her like a baby to a clearing just yards away. Once he set her on the forest bed, he pulled off his shirt and dabbed at her leg to clear some of the blood.

The realization hit him hard, forcing his heart to race into overdrive and his throat to swell in panic.

Blood gushed forth from a gash on her thigh.

It had to be deep. It couldn't be her femoral artery, though. Could it? She'd be dead already, probably.

He knew enough about basic first aid to identify it immediately. His shaking hands worked methodically to tug and tie the flimsy tee-shirt directly onto the wound.

He glanced up at Erica's face, her mouth slightly ajar, the veins in her thin eyelids glowing under transparent skin. Ben lifted her leg onto his shoulder, assessing the tourniquet and gash to see that the spillage had stopped. At least, for now. He shoved both arms back under her, lifting her small body up and moving it close to a fallen log. There, he propped her leg as he searched his pockets for the damn baby wipes. He'd made fun of Erica for keeping baby wipes in her purse. The boys had long outgrown that phase. But she insisted they came in handy in a pinch.

This was most definitely a pinch.

Trembling still, Ben studied his wife's face as he tore two wipes from the pouch. Her color was still grim, and her lips seemed bluish now. He laid the wipes around the wound and took a moment to check her pulse. Swallowing hard, he pushed his thumb into her neck to the left of her throat.

Nothing.

He moved closer, cupping her head in the crook of his arm. He shook his hand out, forcing himself to calm down before pressing two fingers onto the other side of her throat.

He held his breath and forced himself to be utterly still.

A moment passed, then two.

He moved his fingers a hair higher, his nostrils flaring and his eyes searching hers.

And there it was. A dull beat throbbed slowly under the pad of his middle finger. He could sob with relief as the sensation reminded him of the first time he felt the new baby kick, just months earlier.

Had it not yet been a year since they'd learned Erica was pregnant? His mouth pulled into a grimace and he shook his head.

No wonder Erica was still depressed. A lot had happened in fewer than twelve months. He couldn't have expected her to just move on.

But that was exactly what he did. He wanted her onboard with his career move. A cross-country move, for that matter. He wanted her on board as he was about to one-up their status. She thought life in Philly was good? How about life with a head coach for a husband?

Ben was so certain it would fix Erica. Make her happy again. After all, she'd loved living the high life in Pennsylvania. Wasn't that all she had wanted?

Well, as soon as her pouting intensified, he knew she couldn't get over the baby. Which was why he'd ordered the necklace. Closure.

In fact, it was closure mostly for him.

Now, as he held his wife's nearly lifeless head in his arm, he touched the angel pendant, acutely aware of the fragility of life. He'd lost his daughter.

The fragility, too, of marriage.

He'd almost lost his wife once this week. He couldn't lose her again.

Chapter 32: Bo

Once they learned that Harry was a lazy creep worthy of a fine, any lingering suspicion surrounding Bo vanished. And, she didn't need to hang out at the airport anymore. So, she and Anna left with Keegan, who had already interviewed Ben's family.

The prevailing theory was clear: despite the divorce, Ben was preoccupied enough with his father's health that he did not likely kidnap Erica. The FAA was monitoring the air. Border Patrol had a heads up, too. But the smartest move was to canvas the flight path. Keegan would be teaming up with officials from the Bureau of Indian Affairs to allow for a search that would begin beyond the town limits of Maplewood, starting with the reservation and extending indefinitely in the directions of Globe, Safford, and Lake Roosevelt. The search bases were setting up, and Keegan needed to head to the BIA to establish communication there and draw in their resources. He welcomed Bo and Anna to join him.

This investigation could very well boil down to begging for more resources, unless Erica and Ben were found very, very soon. But search efforts north of Tucson and south of Globe held little promise. The frequent updates were a static mess of "No sign, yets" and "Will update soons" and "How's it looking up theres."

Bo heaved a sigh as she pulled herself into the back seat of Keegan's state-issued 1998 Chevy Suburban. On one hand, Bo felt an inexplicable rage that Maplewood couldn't update its damn fleet. On the other, the homey familiarity of a worn-in SUV assured her. Sometimes, it was the old stuff that worked best. She realized, as she pulled the leather strap across her lap, that she was looking for omens anywhere and everywhere. And right now, she had to ignore the bad ones.

Once they were out of the airport parking lot, Carl, Keegan's right-hand man, switched on the sirens. At their flash and blare, Anna covered Bo's hand, squeezing as a tear dropped onto her lap. The lights and noise only heightened their fears, leaving them to sit in silence on the fast ride to Apache tribal headquarters.

Thankfully, the offices were not far from the search headquarters. Bo had half a mind to tear away from the foursome and haul herself out into the woods, slashing at branches and tree trunks as she hunted for her sister. It had been just over a day, and if they had survived the crash, then they'd still be alive and well.

Instead of following her gut instinct this time, she set her jaw and climbed out of the SUV, following Anna and the men as they walked up the concrete steps toward a brick building, outside of which stood two men.

The four men all nodded at each other as Keegan and Carl stopped on the landing, leaving little room for Anna or Bo to join.

Immediately and as if on cue, Anna burst forth in sobs, her body melting into Bo's. It was alarming to everyone, and especially the oldest sister.

"Pull it together, Anna," Bo hissed through her sister's reddish waves. Surprisingly, the admonishment did the trick, and Anna choked out a last sob as Keegan introduced himself and Carl.

"We know who you are. We're sorry to hear about the tragedy," the older official replied. Bo braced herself against the word and was about to correct him, but Keegan opened himself toward her waving his hand at the huddled girls and cutting everyone off.

"We hope it's not a tragedy, yet, Elder."

The two nodded again at Keegan before continuing. "You are welcome to search wherever and however you need in order to bring your loved ones home unharmed. The BIA will cooperate and support your mission to the best of our ability. Our officers will meet you at the search base, wherever you decide it needs to be. We can offer our resources, too." The man paused, and Keegan broke in, offering his hand to both officials.

"Thank you so much, sir. We appreciate it. I'm not sure if our field office informed you before we got here, but the plane likely left Tucson and flew over Globe on its way here. We are looking at the most direct flight path and fanning out from there. We have a location pinpointed for a base camp for the search party. I can have Officer Bellows call you with the mile marker shortly."

With that, they departed the office building and sped down the road another five miles, pulling up to an easement already peppered with vehicles and ATVs and dirt bikes.

Bo assumed that approval was a given, they just had to obtain a verbal green light. Finally, for the first time in hours, her stomach seemed to settle and her pulse slowed to a normal beat. Keegan put the Suburban into park, but before getting out he held a hand up.

"Hang on, ladies. I need to call a local cop to radio in the location. Just sit tight," he directed.

Anna brushed a strand of hair out of her eyes and leaned forward, pulling Keegan's seat back with her, slightly. "Aren't *you* a local cop?" She pointed out.

He ignored her, speaking into the radio.

Moments later, Officer Engelhard had confirmed that the BIA was en route and the press release had just wrapped up. Margaret and her daughters-in-law along with Ben's sisters and mother had been present, tearfully begging for help with the search. They needn't have begged, however. People would have shown up out of sheer boredom, probably. Hundreds of volunteers would be expected over the next few hours.

If one thing became clear during all this: it was that Maplewood folks stuck together and helped each other.

Carl opened the door for Bo and she pushed out, the cool breeze from earlier that day now replaced by a stillness in the air. Bo pulled out her phone, glancing down to catch the time. It was nearly three in the afternoon. She had wasted all day driving and sitting in the airport. Then, her mind fell back to the day before, when she had brushed aside Mary's fears. Shame on Bo. If only she were more like Mary, then Ben and Erica would be safely driving up to Maplewood, arriving right on time to find out that Ben's dad was alive and was expected to have a full recovery.

Bo's eyes adjusted through the afternoon rays as Mary, Robbie, Alan, and their dad rushed up to greet Anna and her. The family fell into a group hug and whispered *I love yous*.

Bo pushed back, finding Mary's gaze. "I'm sorry I didn't take you more seriously, Mare," Bo offered, her hands falling to her sides, helplessly.

Mary, bless her heart, replied with a half-smile and a shrug before Kurt came up behind her, his hand bracing the small of her back. "Hon, your mom is on the phone. She's on her way, but she's stopping for food and drinks for everyone. Do you want to talk to her?"

"No, just tell her thanks." Mary's voice was uncharacteristically commanding. Bo swallowed and looked beyond them toward the others who were starting to group up as another stranger gathered them together, his arms waving everyone in to pay attention.

The next fifteen minutes felt surreal. It was just like true crime TV shows. Clear directions spilled forth from this seasoned search organizer. He was even privy to the fact that Margaret Delaney was on her way with refreshments. His most pervasive advice stuck with Bo: don't make matters worse. It's what Bo had struggled with her whole life. She was always making matters worse. But out here, if a search party member passed out or got lost, it would water down the investigation and could prevent Erica and Ben from being rescued in time.

In time.

Bo had taken it for granted that they could already be dead. But now, a realization hit her. Not only was she to blame for sending Erica and Ben off in a piece of crap plane, but she was also to blame for stalling the search by waving off Mary's concerns.

Not only was she a bad sister. Maybe she was also a bad person.

Chapter 33: Ben

Ben took stock of the situation. They'd been walking for a few hours when Erica fell, which had to put them several miles from the crash. Not good.

Once he had her propped as comfortably as possible and after checking her pulse another dozen times, he was satisfied that her condition was as stable as he could make it. He took another wet wipe and cleared away dried blood that had started to crust around the tourniquet. He didn't want to disrupt it, but he did need to assess the gash. At this rate, it might make sense for them to stay there. They weren't too far from the crash, and if search crews found the plane, they would find Ben and Erica. There was little use in trying to make more progress, at that point, as long as search came soon.

But that's precisely what worried Ben. If search was going to come soon, they'd have been found by then. What if no one was looking for them? What if they assumed Ben and Erica took off for a vacation or something? Worry gnawed on his heart, but he had to push forward, even in small ways.

For now, that meant getting a better look at Erica's wound.

Slowly, he loosened the tee-shirt, awaiting a rush of blood. When none came, he more confidently peeled back the fabric to reveal the injury. It was a gash. A deep one. The fact that she was still alive confirmed for him that she had missed her femoral artery.

Thank God.

Gently, he dabbed the surrounding skin with the fresh wipe, clearing away blood and bits of dirt. Once the skin was mottled pink rather than rust red, he refastened the shirt and pushed back onto his heels, a hand holding him in place as he looked back to where she fell.

He'd thought for sure she'd fallen directly onto a broken-off branch that poked out from a downed tree trunk. But no bark or twigs appeared along the wound. No branch was sticking out from her thigh.

Curious, Ben stood from her side and retraced his steps to where she fell. There, he combed the area, finding no obvious branch or twig or even a sharp-sided rock. Then, as he took one step closer, it appeared. A piece of rebar, one end rammed into the earth, the other poking through pine needles, entirely camouflaged by the earth tones.

Visible dried blood proved it. Erica had the terrible luck of falling and catching her inner thigh on someone's leftover building materials. He bent closer to examine the rod, praying he wouldn't find rust. Then, another thing dawned on him.

Rebar...

People.

People had been here. He stood, searching around himself frantically. Maybe they were closer to civilization than he realized. Or at least, they had to be near campgrounds. Maybe even some homesteads or tribal housing. As he took in the area, he noted tree stumps—forestation. Good.

But that was it. No other litter. No campfires. No nearby clearings of any human-made kind. Still, he now had hope that someone would discover them before he had to make the decision to move Erica in her delicate condition.

Ben took in a deep breath and trudged back to Erica's spot. He felt utterly helpless. He checked her pulse again, finding it more easily this time. The tee-shirt worked well at stopping the blood, and she seemed to be improving. Her coloring even looked warmer. He'd now have to pray that tetanus wouldn't become an immediate concern. Or infection. Beyond that, she'd need water at the least. Food, less so. He thought about how long it had been since they crashed.

He glanced up to the sky, holding a hand over his eyes as he gauged the sun. It wasn't at its highest point any longer. It must be some time after noon. He spun in a circle before crumpling down beside Erica and leaning up against the log. He was confused and thirsty and worried.

They couldn't stay there if he hoped to revive her. He needed to find water, of course, but he was now also confident he might find help. If they were close enough for people to litter, then they were close enough for rescue. He licked his lips and held his head down to Erica, listening as her breath came in through her nose and out through her mouth, breaks here and there. It wasn't as steady as he'd like. He moved back, examining her perfect, porcelain face, tainted by dashes of dirt and sprays of dried blood from the plane windshield. Here, in the woods, after asking for a divorce, after crashing in a plane, after making up with her husband, she lay. He had to do more for her.

He closed his eyes and kissed her forehead before running a thumb along her sunken cheek.

"Eri, I'll be right back. Stay here," he whispered and then rose to his feet, clapping dirt and debris from his butt. He looked around, deciding to stay north. He'd walk only until he couldn't see her any longer, then he'd move in circles, counting his paces and eyeing her position. It was too risky to lose sight of his wife, but he had to take the chance of finding help.

With a pit growing in his stomach, he left her there, leg draped over a massive trunk, sandaled foot dangling, red toenails flashing as he made his way on, looking back every few feet.

Chapter 34: Erica

Rustling. Laughter. It sounded far away and nearby. Erica squeezed her eyes shut harder. *Go away*, she thought, her head throbbing, lips cracked, throat dry. She tried to swallow, hardly able. Licking her lips made everything worse. The thirst was overwhelming. Then came nausea.

More laughter. Now closer.

Tentatively, she lifted an eyelid, grimacing as though any slight movement would knock her back out.

Was she knocked out?

Her eyeball roamed down along her body, and she took in the tee-shirt around her leg, accounting for the distinct numb feeling that seemed to make up the entire left side of her body. Her leg was crooked up on a big log, and pine needles and dirt matted her hair.

She closed her eyes again, breathing slowly, forcing her heart to slow down.

Again, laughter.

Both her eyes flashed open and she twisted her head around her, seeing no one.

"*Ben*," she whispered.

No response.

Sounds grew from afar, and she froze, listening for Ben's voice amongst them. Slowly, she pushed up from the ground, propping her elbows behind her. From there, she could see over the log and into the endless woods.

No one.

She held still, listening. Again, a faint chorus of laughter. But it was dying out. Leaving her. Moving farther away.

"*Ben!*" She called out, but her voice croaked from within, resulting in a hoarse murmur. She shifted her weight forward and lifted her bandaged leg up and off the tree in order to stand. But as the leg came down on the ground, pain shot up through the thigh. The tee-shirt loosened around her leg.

She flipped over and pressed up on her hands, pulling her good leg beneath her, but as soon as she moved the weight to her foot, exhaustion brought her back down to the ground in a thud.

Her body felt like it weighed five hundred pounds. Panting now, she collected herself, listening again. Nothing but quiet.

"Hello! Ben?!" She screamed with all her might. And still, her voice fell flat between her rough lips.

With every moment, she became more and more aware of her circumstances.

She fell. She cut her leg. Ben's shirt was wrapped around the cut, now bleeding again, a slow trickle pooling on the ground beneath her, the sticky fluid adhering to her skin errant pine needles and dry soil.

Then, without explanation of any kind, not even a note in the damn dirt, Ben left her there.

Now she was awake, barely, and someone was nearby, unhearing her. She bit down on her lip and pinned her elbows into the earth, one in front of the other as she dragged herself toward the general direction of the voices.

"Ben! Anyone! Help me!" She cried out from her position past the log. "*Help me!*" Her voice was coming back to her with each word until fire scorched her throat and her lips cracked like a desert, fresh blood seeped out, wetting her tongue as she ran it across the thin skin.

She had no tears to cry. Instead, she took a deep breath in and pushed her hands into the earth, pressing up quickly in one swift motion. She forced her good leg under her, crooking the bad one at the knee and hopped once forward, but as she did, her right leg gave out from beneath her, spilling her over a log that happened to frame a sloping hill.

Down she rolled, coming to a stop about a third of the way into a ravine or canyon of some kind. If she had enough energy, she would have crawled back up.

But she didn't. So she lay there. Her eyelids fluttering open and shut with every bird chirp, every gush of wind. Hunger and thirst assailed her as much or more than the pain in her leg. Sheer exhaustion took hold. Until, again, nothing.

Chapter 35: Bo

Before they embarked on the foot search, Dutch had appeared. He was close friends with one of the Apache County Search and Rescue deputies who gave him a rundown of events.

All surrounding counties had deployed resources to support the search, but they were most confident the Air Force would be the entity to eventually detect the plane. The FAA had announced that the aircraft had disappeared from radar somewhere between the empty desert that framed Pinal Peak and Globe. However, at an altitude of 9,000 feet and an approximate speed of 120 miles per hour, the plane could have gone down in a vast expanse of search area. Unfortunately, there had been no flight plan registered (which Bo already knew) and the beacon had never pinged (which Bo also knew). BIA officials were sending volunteers, too, but this group was getting started in small teams right now.

Stepping into the forest alongside Anna, Dutch, Kurt, and Mary, Bo suddenly and wholly felt alone. Alone in her crappy life choices. Alone in her guilt. Alone in pacing through the woods where she grew up and had never wanted to return.

As she picked through pine saplings and twisted juniper trunks, her mind flashed back to her childhood, when she and her brothers and sisters would embark into the forest on adventures.

Back then, she secretly wished she would get lost. To have everyone's worry and concern and attention on her sounded glamorous and cool and fulfilling. Having been the oldest sister, she was often looked upon as a second mother to her younger siblings, encouraged to shepherd them through the grocery market, help bathe them, feed them mushed peas.

By the time she was ten, she'd practically done half the child rearing in the Delaney home, while her mother and father ran the farm and ranch. She could even remember sitting in her little room, the room she shared with each of her sisters at one time or another, lying awake in bed at night, staring up into the darkness as resentment washed over her. Over time, she resolved to live her own life. Of course, that had only resulted in light shoplifting, mediocre vandalism, wild parties, bad boys, and booze- at least, in the short run. In the long run, her bitter attitude got her through a second-rate bachelor's program with no contacts, no friends, and little more than a chip on her shoulder and a notepad in her hand.

From there, all she had was her mind, the same one that floated out into her deepest desires during those little adventures into the woods. The adventures where Erica would play Mom, and Alan would play Dad, and they would boss all the other kids around. Bo would only ever agree to be the horse or a distant wacky cousin. She was so... removed from her siblings and from the game.

It didn't scare her back then. But it scared her a little now. Had her selfish, independent nature resulted in the disappearance of her sister and Ben?

Would it result in their death?

The violent beating of helicopter rotors buzzed overhead, snapping Bo out of it. She had fallen a few steps behind the others.

"Hurry up, Bo," Mary turned to call back. "Stay with us."

She did as she was told, tripping over a root as she strode ahead. What if Erica or Ben had gotten hurt out in the wild? She cleared her throat. "Do you guys think they stayed with the plane?"

Dutch replied, his tone even, "They'd be crazy not to."

"Yeah, but what if they didn't?" Worry pinched Anna's face as she gripped Dutch's bulky arm more tightly.

"Why wouldn't they?" Mary chimed in, ever the voice of reason.

"Ben was so anxious to get home," Bo replied as she pulled her hair into a rubber band that had been strangling her wrist.

Anna threw her a dirty look. "You don't even know if they survived the crash."

Bo ran a hand along her neck, which was slick in cool sweat. Anna's words were harsh. But, she was right. Who knew if Ben and Erica were still alive? What with her luck, she'd trip over the corpse of her own sister. A chill went up her spine and she glanced behind, back to the highway, searching for somebody- anybody- who might be flailing their arms with the good news. *We found them! Stop the search!* In her heart, she was begging God. Pleading with him. *Please, God, please just let them be alive. I'll never make another mistake in my life. I'll go back to church. I'll do anything. Please.*

Chapter 36: Ben

He'd walked for no more than thirty minutes, always taking care to swoop back several paces toward Erica to check on her, in a semi-circle around where she lay. He had to venture out a little farther in order to get a good read on the land, but he never wandered too far from Erica. He wanted to hear her if she rustled awake. The strategy offered him a clear sense of the area and confirmed that the sun was now on its way to set. Soon. He'd found little more than a lone beer can (it could have been a soda can, but that didn't seem quite right) and a depression in the earth that may, at one time, have been a campfire. But there were no ashes remaining to confirm as much. He'd also realized there was a dry basin nearby where Erica had fallen. It was expansive, and he was fairly certain it was the Apache Basin, which had- at one point- been considered a modest canyon. He had somehow missed that as they were hiking together. It was somewhat shallow, but wide and craggy, and he chose not to take the risk of traversing the far side of it, for fear he'd be too far from his wife.

But, they had indeed been traveling north, as he'd thought, and once he completed his 180 degree scouting mission around where Erica lay, he realized he hadn't looped back in to get a peek of her in the last five or ten minutes. He stopped, about two hundred yards northeast of her and propped his hands on his hips, breathing in and out rhythmically, uncertain how to proceed. It was best that he go assess her vitals and then figure it out.

As he turned and began to walk back to his wife, his eyes narrowed on the log where he'd left her.

Erica's slender leg no longer poked over the fallen tree. He squinted harder as he felt his chest rise and fall in hollow breaths. Picking up pace, he knew it couldn't be. She most certainly had to be there.

But he saw nothing. No blonde wisps flying above the log. No red toes bobbing at the end of her wounded leg. His heart fell deep into his chest and broke out in a sprint.

"Erica!" he yelled, his arms pumping as he hurdled over tree stumps and saplings, pinecones kicking up in his wake. "Erica!" he screamed again through the warm afternoon sun, its rays splitting through the trees, casting shadows that distracted him as his eyes searched before he reached her resting spot.

He pulled up at the log and a lump formed in his throat.

She wasn't there.

What the hell?

"Erica!" His voice echoed through the trees, wind carrying it back around to him until he heard a little pip cry out from far, far away.

His panic subsiding, he cupped a hand to his ear, eyes trained down as he strained to hear.

"Ben!" came a soft melody. The voice of an angel. He followed the sound, answering it with his own dry, weak vocals, his lips splitting as he screamed.

"Erica! Where are you!"

Rustling preceded her response. "Right over here! I rolled down!"

He moved past the length of the log and over to the hidden basin before following its slope. A laugh escaped his lips, and his body relaxed, his eyes smiling down at her..

There, not twenty yards away, sat little Erica, hands propped behind her, hair mussed, legs splayed out on the upside of the hill. She looked adorable and terrible all at once. Like a disheveled ragdoll. He dashed down toward her, grabbing her face in his hands as he eased himself onto the hillside next to her.

"I was so scared, Erica," he whispered into her ear before moving his mouth over hers, covering her lips with his before pulling back, staring deeply into her blue eyes. He then examined her face, pressing her hair back from her head, hungry to see that she was alive underneath yesterdays' cuts and today's thirst. "Your lips are so chapped. You feel clammy. What happened? How did you get here?"

He let her begin her story as he scooted back to check on her thigh. She started by describing how she woke up, scared, alone, afraid he'd left her there.

"I didn't leave you here. I wasn't far at all," he replied as he peeked under the shirt to see the wound had bled again and the skin around it turned puffy and red, though he wasn't sure if that was from dried blood or subdural bruising.

"Ow," she tensed and her knee pulled up as he gently pressed the tender skin. She recovered quickly, stretching her leg back out as she continued. "Oh, so that *was* you? I thought I was hallucinating."

"What was me?" he asked, pulling a wet wipe from the pack but tearing it in two and stuffing the other half back inside. They were getting low on wipes now. A twelve-pack travel pouch wouldn't go much further.

"The laughing... or whatever. I heard laughing and talking, I think. I don't know, I was confused. Dizzy."

Ben lifted his hands, eyeing his wife. "You *heard* someone? Like, nearby?"

She nodded innocently. "I'm pretty sure. They must have come in close but then took off. I guess they didn't hear me." Her voice fell an octave, matching her chin as it dipped to her chest.

He pushed up from the ground, his head whipping around in all directions. "Hello!" he called out. "Help!" The word crashed through his throat, catching on his lips as he jogged up the hill and scanned the woods. "HELP US!"

He skipped back down the hill, grabbing Erica by her shoulders. "You *heard someone*? Are you *positive*?" he demanded.

Her shoulders quaked beneath his hands as she nodded, her eyebrows nipped together and her mouth ajar. "I'm, I'm sorry." It came out scratchy and pathetic. His hope turned to frustration. Frustration to rage.

"Erica, someone was here and you didn't... you didn't get their attention?"

"Ben, I don't know," she wailed, covering her face in her hands. Through sobs she tried to explain herself. Something about being confused. Thinking it was him. Trying to cry out but her voice wouldn't work.

It was all excuses, as far as he could tell. Scared and angry, he stood back up and crossed his arms, looking down on her from above. "This is all your fault, Erica. If you weren't so obsessed with 'feelings' I'd never have been distracted in that damn plane." His air quotes turned to a finger pointing back the way they came.

She cried harder now, offering no reply.

He dropped back down beside her, wrapping her in his arms and moving his mouth to her ear, his jawline damp from her sparse tears. "I'm sorry. I didn't mean it. I'm sorry, babe," he cooed to her, rocking her back and forth and realizing, with his cheek pressed firmly to her temple, that she was burning up.

Chapter 37: Erica

"We're still so far from the highway, Ben. Why not just head back to the plane? Maybe the bears won't come back," she pleaded with him through her misery, feeling weaker by the minute and colder, too. The sun, by now, was beginning to dip below the top of the trees. They had little time left in the day. Bear-infested shelter was better than no shelter. Wasn't exposure just as likely?

"Erica, you stabbed yourself on rebar. We are close to something. Look around you- all these tree stumps? See the red spray paint on those trunks over there? Logging. We can definitely get *somewhere* tonight. I can't defend us against a family of black bears, especially if I don't have your help."

Erica heaved rasps of breaths. His ridiculous paranoia could cost them their lives. "Do you really think they would attack us?" She shivered and ran her hands up and down her arms, eyeing Ben's bare chest and abs. "Aren't you cold, anyway?" Her voice was quieter. Her teeth chattered, too, making it hard to talk. Ben knelt down by her side, reaching for her hands and rubbing them together in his.

"Babe, you might have a fever. We can't wait for rescue. We have to be our own rescue team. Listen, I am confident I can carry you for a ways. It'll be uncomfortable, and we need to be mindful of your wound. If it starts bleeding…" his voice trailed off as she held a hand up to his mouth to shush him.

"Let's just stay here, Benny. I don't want to move." He rubbed his free hand over his face, taking a deep breath.

"You need help *now*, Erica," his glance down to her thigh revealed something in his eyes. A worry that rooted deeper than just the infection. Why had it come on so fast? What could it mean? Tetanus or the like would take days to set in. He prayed to God it wasn't blood poisoning.

"What?" She pinned him with a glare. "Ben, do you think I'm going to die?" A different fear settled in her stomach. One that hadn't risen when Ben had patted the back of his hand across her damp forehead, declaring her hot. Her face flattened and her breath caught in her throat as she awaited his answer. "*Ben?*" she whispered.

"I don't know, Eri. I don't know if you'll die or be totally fine or get worse. But, I do know that we can hike, together. You on my back or shoulders. It'll be slow going, but it's our only answer. We have come too far from the plane regardless of the bears. We are near civilization. We have a chance. We have to take it."

In that moment, Erica could see what coaches, and managers, and players saw in Ben Stevens. He wasn't afraid to be brave. For everyone. His pep talk was equal parts honest and hopeful, cautious and inspiring. She trusted him. She licked her lips, momentarily wetting the dry sky as she looked up at him, a tiny smile pricking her mouth. "Okay, Coach. Tell me what to do." Her voice had turned breathy and barren, and her leg was now throbbing despite the tightly wound t-shirt. Any numbing effects had long since vanished, so now that they had their plan, she accepted it. Sitting on the side of that basin in pain and cold sounded no better than bumping along on Ben's shoulders, each misstep jarring the crap out of her.

And that's exactly how it went. He hauled her, firefighter style, across his shoulders, her stomach pinned against his neck, legs stacked on his right shoulder. Ben's hand gripped the inner thigh on the good leg. His left hand held in place her arm. Pain shot through her body as he positioned her firmly against his bare skin.

She was freezing. Her flesh stood on ends as she clung with her free hand onto his bicep, desperate to hold herself as still as was possible.

He took a tentative first step before asking, "Are you okay up there?"

"Not really, but what choice do I have?" she answered with a cough. He didn't laugh, and neither did she. Instead, she winced with every step, finally crying out in pain when they had walked no more than ten feet. "Ben, stop, please!" She whispered down to him. He held still, speaking to her through gritted teeth.

"Erica, I cannot make you any more comfortable. Just hang in there okay?"

She began to weep, miniature dry sobs rocking her further into pain. She forced herself to stop out of the agony.

"Erica," he said, his voice soft, kind. "You are the strongest, toughest woman I know. If anyone can handle this, it's you. I don't want to carry you on piggyback, because your leg could start bleeding again. Same if I put you on shoulders like I hold the boys."

The last word shocked her into compliance.

The boys.

She had to suck it up for them. She had to make it home to her two sons. The center of her universe. She refused to leave them motherless. She inhaled a breath deep into her chest and grunted in reply. "Okay. Go."

For the first hour, Erica vacillated between cold and pain, pain and cold. She couldn't tell which was worse: the horrid chills and periodic nausea or the throbbing. Ben stopped very rarely, and only for a moment, carrying on like their lives depended on his forward motion. She supposed that it did.

Then, somewhere after an hour of their shared silence, she realized she didn't feel pain anymore. And soon after that, a heavy exhaustion replaced the chills. Hardly able to keep her eyes open, despite the bleeding sun that hung wearily above the horizon, she finally succumbed to sleep, if only for a moment.

Ben's booming voice frightened her awake.

"Erica, wake up," he commanded from above. Her eyes fluttered open to see that he was standing over her, patting her cheek and pressing a thumb to her jugular.

"What?" she squinted up at him, through the dusky sky. She vaguely realized she was lying on the earth, now, Ben kneeling beside her. All she felt was thirst. Awful, awful thirst. If only she could suck on an ice cube, like she did when she was in labor with the boys. Or even just a sip of water. Anything to quench the urgent need. Her eyes heavy, it was near impossible to keep them open.

"Erica," he hissed, shaking her shoulders until she opened her eyes again. He grabbed her jaw in his hand and turned her head slowly. "Look! A house!"

Chapter 38: Bo

Hours later, Bo, Mary, Anna, Dutch, and Kurt had rejoined the rest of the volunteer search party at the search base. ATVs and helicopters continued to refuel and deploy.

Bo didn't understand it. How big of a search area was this? How had no one seen *anything*? Not a trace?

Now, as she huddled next to her mom and dad for warmth, Keegan approached them, the glow from his flashlight bobbing out on the ground in front of him. Shivers tickled Bo's back and she wrapped her arms around herself as she wondered how cold Erica must be in nothing more than a flimsy yoga outfit. Even Ben was only wearing a shirt and shorts, she'd recalled. Here Bo stood, in jeans and one of her brothers' sweatshirts, and she was more than moderately uncomfortable. Her mind flicked to the twins, restlessly watching TV with Mary now, back at her lodge. Mary felt compelled to spin it into a summer camp for them, doing her best to distract the little boys from somber family members and frantic news coverage.

"Mr. Delaney? Mrs. Delaney?" Keegan nodded at Bo's parents before touching her elbow. She moved aside, opening their little circle to the tall detective.

Dick Delaney's expression turned long as he focused his eyes on Keegan. Margaret rubbed her eyes and frowned. It was the only response he was going to get at that moment.

Keegan cleared his throat. "Obviously, it being dark and whatnot, it's best for volunteers to consider heading home for the night. We're still running crews. The search effort isn't stopping. Just might be safer to call it a night for those of you on foot here."

Margaret began to reply, her eyebrows crooked into the beginnings of anger, but Keegan held up a hand. "But I know you won't hear of it. So I spoke with Alan," Bo suddenly recalled that Keegan and Alan knew each other fairly well. Maybe they'd even been friends? She was too tired to remember. It wasn't even that late, but emotional exhaustion had dug roots behind her eyes, where her brain had begun to throb in an early headache. "His wife is gon' bring down some tents and another meal. He just got off the phone with her. We can't let you go out and continue to search, but we can let you camp out with us," he flicked a glance to Bo, who'd begun nodding vigorously.

"That's perfect, right Mom and Dad?" All Dick and Margaret could do in return was nod solemnly. Keegan pointed beyond them and gave them further directions about charging their phones, just to be on the safe side. They wanted to keep lines of communication open. Just in case.

As he went to leave, Bo reached a hand up to his shoulder.

"Keegan?" She searched his eyes through the starlit sky.

They softened, and he turned to face her fully.

"Are you going out in there to search or do you have to stay here, too?"

A quizzical expression emerged, and he replied that he was stationed there but was flexible. "Bo," he went on. "I have one job: to find your sister. I don't leave until we do. I give you my word on that."

She forced a small smile, but instead it felt like her face was fracturing. "Well, I know I won't sleep. Neither will any of my family. We can't just sit here all night waiting and wondering if they're alive. Keegan," she put a hand on his chest, but he didn't flinch. "Keegan, can you ride me out there? To keep looking?"

He covered her hand in his, breathed in and finally out before looking past her up toward the line of ATVs and dirt bikes sitting unused by the volunteers who chose to go get some shuteye.

"I need to call my field office and check in on the credit card and cell reports- to see if anything's hit so far. After that, yes. Hang tight."

As he brushed past her, Bo stood, facing the edge of the forest in which she prayed she was about to find Erica and Ben- deep in the maze of the Apache reservation land.

Anna joined Bo. "You're gonna go in? Just be safe. I can't stand to lose two of you," she said as she wrapped an arm around her older sister.

Bo turned, not bothering to lift her arms in reciprocation. "Don't you all want to go? I mean, it's so desperate."

"Well, yeah. Robbie is boarding a helicopter right now."

Bo twisted around, craning her neck to look at the few lingering faces left. "Where? What do you mean?"

"Not here. He's at the airport. He's going up with an air rescue team as a spotter." Alan is taking off with Carl to head east. They're gonna set up another base there and start a foot search at the break of dawn.

Bo pulled her phone out of the pocket of Robbie's hoodie. She loved wearing her brothers' clothes. Always had. There was a certain hominess to it. This particular one had been an old favorite of hers.

He'd gotten it as a Christmas gift one year, but she was pretty certain her mom found it at a thrift store. Across the chest it read, **DON'T HASSLE ME, I'M LOCAL**. It was from a movie or something, and the whole family had adopted it as their mantra. The tourist population in Maplewood had its ups and downs, but to the locals who benefitted only marginally from the influx of visitors, tourists were never welcome. Only irritating.

The stained sweatshirt, with its threadbare cuffs and specks of dried paint splashed across the front, reminded her of her upbringing. Hard work. Grunt labor. Always a project. Always something else to stress about and work on. Lately, of course, ever since they shut the farm and ranch down and all that was left was Margaret's garden and a modest chicken coop, life was probably different. Alan and Robbie were making good money running their outdoor bar and keeping up with the orchard. Now, tourists were a big part of their income. The Delaneys couldn't well complain about them anymore.

By the time Keegan had returned, Dutch came by to pull Anna away toward a tent that was going up. They planned to camp out, though it was ridiculous to set up a tent. Who would sleep?

A morbid thought swelled in Bo's head. Two people who very well could be sleeping at that particular moment. She rubbed her eyes and squashed it. Forcing herself to think positively. Ben and Erica were alive. And, she genuinely hoped they were in a safe place where they could rest. After all, they were going on Day 3 of their disappearance. They may just need some sleep.

Keegan strode back down the slight slope toward her. "Okay, Bo. We'll take an ATV. If you've got your phone on you or anything else, tuck it somewhere safe. Two other crew members are joining us on a second vehicle. Never travel alone."

He didn't wait for her to follow. She nearly had to jog to keep up with his long strides. "Keegan, what about the cell phone or credit cards? Any hits?"

"No," he spat.

Obvious, but she still needed to hear every detail she could get her hands on.

Moments later, they were straddling a four-wheeler, helmets adding some small warmth in the quickly cooling evening. She leaned forward and wrapped her arms around Keegan's trim midsection.

"Hold on!" He shouted back over the roar of the little engine. And away they went. The other ATV was leading them. Its passenger holding out a small laminated map of some sort. She had no idea what the strategy was. Hopefully they weren't just retracing another search team's path through the woods. Maybe that explained the map.

The seat vibrated between her legs, and wind blasted by as they whizzed through trees and around stumps. Bo's hair slapped against her face, sticking to her wet lips. With each sensation, a new layer of fear settled in her gut.

She stared into the woods, worried they were moving too fast to see anything. She remembered the flashlight in her hoodie pocket. Kurt had handed it to her as she boarded the ATV. Now, she pulled it out, gripping Keegan tighter with her left hand. She clicked it on and flashed it along the trees. Totally useless. She could see hardly anything with the dinky light as wilderness blurred by.

Why were they moving so fast? They were gonna miss something for sure. She clicked off the light and shoved it back into her pocket through the bumpy ride. After a few moments more she squeezed Keegan and yelled into his ear, "Shouldn't we slow down? We might miss something!"

Without turning his head he answered, "This area has already been covered! We're en route to a new section."

She settled back, some degree of ease washing through her. Okay, so this wasn't a vanity mission to shut her up. They were heading deeper into the forest. Much, much deeper.

For the next half an hour or so, Bo kept quiet, her head cocked to Keegan's right, eyes trained ahead. They'd seen nothing of interest. Not even litter. Abruptly, the ATV pulled to a stop, its rear passenger hopping off and striding over.

"Hey, boss," he called. "We're 20 miles in. Goal is 60 for this mission, but we are gonna head east and cover new terrain, a narrow strip on the other side of Apache Basin. Is she okay back there?" The man pointed to Bo who threw him a thumbs up. *Good. Take her all the way*, she thought to herself. She'd go a million miles left, right, forward, backward, sideward... if it meant she could see her sister.

This would mean another couple hours of riding, and she was glad for it. She felt like, for the first time in her life, she was doing the right thing, even if it was the result of a bad decision. One step at a time to fixing her life. She heaved a sigh in and out and repositioned her head behind Keegan's back, shutting her eyes for just a moment.

It hadn't yet been an hour, when again, the ATV in front careened to the side, stopping dramatically and kicking up dust in its wake. Bo couldn't help but roll her eyes behind Keegan. Just go, already. What, were they out of gas? Then, Keegan stood, nearly knocking her back off the seat. Confused, it took her a moment to right herself and press off the ATV. Keegan stepped back, holding his hand out for her to grab as they looked ahead, into a thicket of cracked tree trunks and splayed branches...

The plane.

Chapter 39: Ben

Well, it wasn't a house, per se. It was a trailer. But that didn't matter, because it was *something*. He lifted Erica from the ground, talking to her as he paced toward the dwelling.

"Stay awake, Erica, we're almost there. We're gonna be okay, you just gotta stay with me." And then, "*Hello! Help us!*" he yelled through a clearing in the trees as they neared the dumpy shack. His eyes searched the two windows, cracked blinds doing a poor job of offering any privacy.

No lights, but it wasn't quite dark. Just getting close. His eyes followed another clearing to the right of the property, if you could call it that, which led out to a narrow, overgrown path through the trees. Small fir trees emerged from the earthen road, hiding any signs of tire tracks.

Erica's eyes fluttered closed and he shook her in his arms. "Erica wake up, dammit, we're safe. We're here!"

She stirred, a moan escaping her pale lips. His bare chest was slick with sweat, despite the dropping temperature, and he couldn't tell where his overexertion ended and her clammy fever began. Her skin was hot on his arms, but he pushed forward over stumps and through weeds.

The box of a house sank into the ground and no patio or walkway bled forth from the front door which, at one point, hung above the ground some inches. Now, it was flush with the forest floor.

"*Hello! Help us!*" He called over his wife's hot, limp body. He kept moving, his eyes on the windows and door for signs of life.

Nothing.

He pulled up to the door and called once more through the thin aluminum, hoping to wake someone, anyone. Quietly, he pressed his ear against the tin, listening for movement.

"Okay, Erica. Wake up." He shook her body until she shivered and moved her arms over her chest. "Erica, I need to set you down," he spoke to her slowly as he bent down and rested her body to the right of the door, which he tore open like an animal, finding a second door behind it, hollow core. He violently shook the knob before throwing all of his weight into it, busting through on the first try.

"*Hello! We need help! Is anyone in here?*" His voice fell off as his eyes adjusted to the dark space. It was immediately clear that no one had been in the trailer in some time. Months, at least. A thick layer of dust coated every vertical surface, even the matted shag carpet puffed under Ben's footfall. *Damn.*

He slapped open the aluminum screen door and stepped out and over to Erica, whose body he hefted up. It felt somehow heavier now, but she was awake. Aware.

"What's going on, Ben?" She groaned as he squeezed them both through the doorway and into the musty trailer.

"No one's here, but we have a shelter, Erica. We can probably stay the night here." He eyed a sagging couch along the far wall and carried Erica to it, inspecting it before gently laying her into the sinking cushions and propping her leg on the arm. There. That would be a good spot for now. He held a hand to her head. She was still hot, and droplets were breaking down her temples. "Erica, you have to stay awake. You do not have a choice. Do you understand me?"

She nodded faintly, licking her lips. "Water," she whispered.

"Okay, hang on. I'm gonna look around. Just, keep your eyes open, whatever you do." Tentatively, he padded from the living room onto the cracked linoleum floor of the kitchen. A square of dirt outlined where a fridge once sat. He muttered a curse and moved to the sink where he tested the faucet.

Rust-colored spray choked out and sputtered off. He pumped the handles several more times, but nothing else came. He slammed his fist onto the counter, knocking over a box of baking soda from which nothing spilled. He grabbed the box and peered inside. A layer of powder shimmied along the top of a white brick as he shook the box.

He tossed it back down onto the counter, glancing along the empty space to see nothing more than a dry-rotted sponge. Turning his attention to the two cabinets above the sink, he slapped them open. A bag of crusty, yellowed marshmallows—the underside of the bag had melted onto the corkboard shelf, leaving the rest of the plastic package to mold to the hard confectionary cubes.

In the second cabinet sat a roach motel, around which lay a few roaches on their backs. Splinters that were once little cockroach feet encircled the carcasses as though they'd been shocked off their legs.

"Erica!" he hollered over his shoulder to check on her. A muffled *yeah* drifted into the kitchen as he bent down to pull open the drawers and bottom cabinets, finding a stray plastic grocery bag and nothing else. The kitchen had been completely emptied. It was any wonder that a couch still sat in the living room, rotting through the floor. A barren breakfast nook offered no hope, either, and he stalked back out to the living room, pressing the back of his hand against her head again, praying that the fever would somehow break on its own. That her body would step up and kill the infection off.

Still no luck. She felt the same as moments earlier.

"Be right back," he growled and turned to scour the bathroom. The type of person who'd leave a trailer to rot in the middle of the woods wouldn't likely stock a first aid kit or rubbing alcohol. But he had to look.

The door was swollen shut, forcing Ben to punch it open with his shoulder. It swung into the small space, the doorknob cracking against the wall. Ben stepped up to the sink, flipping the faucet to check for anything. Not even rust this time. He looked up, into the mirror and nearly jumped at his reflection. What he saw there was not the man he knew. Smudges of dirt, sweat-slicked hair, and bloodshot eyes did little to distract from his cracked lips and sallow complexion or the smattering of cuts on his forehead and nose. He looked nearly as bad as Erica, and yet she was in much worse shape. His eyes flashed to the boys, how scared they must be. And then to his relationship with them. How little time they'd spent together.

Despite the move and the promotion- two things he wanted more desperately than anything- the Stevens household was not the picture-perfect family he had thought he'd built. In fact, it was the exact opposite. He shook his head, shame reddening his neck, and then flipped open the medicine cabinet, resolving then and there to change things. As soon as he got home. He would make a change.

As the mirrored door crashed open, a deluge of hypodermic needles dropped from the shallow shelves into the pink porcelain sink. All packaged, thankfully.

Still, Ben fell back into the door. His mind leapt to drugs. For sure, had to be drug paraphernalia. Yet, wouldn't there be signs in the kitchen? Pots, pans, foil...? Whatever. Didn't matter, because he was totally and thoroughly freaked out. He dropped to the lower cabinet, half-expecting some rabid animal to jump out. No. Just a half-used toilet paper roll, crepe-y and yellower than the marshmallows.

Shutting the doors he scanned the tub to see a rusty dollar-store razor and withered washcloth dried to the bottom. He blew a heavy sigh through his lips, feeling his thirst now more than ever.

A walk-through of the bedroom revealed a dingy box spring and a few slats of wood. This place sucked. But it was shelter. Now he had to decide between awaiting rescue in this relatively safe location and doubling down on hiking out of the woods.

As he strolled back to the living room, watching shivers wrack his wife's body, her gray lips opening and closing in waves of pain, he knew the answer.

Ben Stevens would have to save his wife by himself.

Chapter 40: Bo

Bo pushed past Keegan toward the plane, dodging branches and hurdling roots instinctively as she flew. She zigzagged in front of the ATV headlights, shadows cutting in and out of her path as she sprinted.

"*Erica!*" Her screams burned through her throat. "*Erica!*" Oh, God. Please be there. Oh, God. "*Erica! Ben!*"

She was at the nose of the plane in an instant, her hands and legs shaking uncontrollably. She felt Keegan and the other two join her there with floodlight style flashlights. They split to either side of the cockpit. She followed Keegan to the passenger side, steeling herself for what may lie within.

She swallowed hard, her nostrils flaring, her breath shallow, as Keegan popped the handle and pulled open the door for her to see.

Blood. Everywhere. It looked like a freaking murder scene, especially under the bright glare of the lights. She glanced up at Keegan, who was moving around the door slowly to get a better look inside.

"Stay here," he commanded with a firm palm against her shoulder. She swatted it away and grabbed his arm for leverage, pulling herself into the seat and thrusting her head to the back compartment.

Nothing.

A breath escaped her lips. *Thank God. Thank you, God. Thank you, God, Thank you, God.*

She twisted on the leather seat, dried blood flaking off under her fingers. "They're alive. They aren't here, they're alive," she stuttered to the three men, who did little more than nod in response as they began a methodical examination of the mess.

"Bo, get the hell out, we have to work this now." Keegan's voice was cold and harsh, but she did as she was told, following one of the other men as he cased the area outside the plane. Keegan jogged back to the ATV, holding the radio up to his mouth and calling in the details. Bo wondered how her parents would take the news. It all boiled down to one word: hope. They had it. They had hope. And if they did, then so did Ben and Erica.

Bo continued screaming her sister's name into the twilight, waiting with each call to hear a reply, but only ever hearing her own voice echo back.

She passed her flashlight over the front of the plane and to the sides of its damaged nose and then saw black leather peek out from under the wing. "Hey! Look!" she cried. The officer on the other side of the wing stood from the ground and held up a duffle bag, its fabric flapping open in shards. Bo pulled out the purse. Erica's purse. Ben's duffle. They looked as if they'd been run through a paper shredder.

"Did the crash do that?"

"No, Keegan's voice came from behind her. In fact, this isn't much of a crash at all. Seems like they did a good job of gliding her down. The trees probably helped."

"Then what's up with the blood? The bags?" Bo held a helpless hand out toward the evidence.

As if on cue, the man who'd been combing near the duffle surfaced from the dark forest floor with the carcass of a massive goose hanging upside down, its rubbery feet pinched between his fingers.

Bo stared at the dead bird, mentally calculating what happened. Just as she opened her mouth to guess, Keegan interjected. "Bird blasted the windshield out and they glided down here. Average footpace is three miles an hour. Fit couple, might make it five miles an hour over time." He stalled, computing the numbers in his head. "We need to radio back; that makes for a fairly expansive search radius, but it's reasonable to assume they headed north. We can focus that way while we mobilize the rest of the team from this location."

He jogged back to the ATV and Bo followed at his heels while the other two loaded theirs and revved the engine. Keegan repeated his thoughts over radio and relief washed through Bo. She just knew they'd find them. Ben was smart and so was Erica. And they were both in great shape, that was true. They'd stay north. No reason not to. But why had they left to begin with?

She yelled her question into Keegan's ear as he turned the ignition.

"Who knows- maybe he thought they were close to the highway?"

A worry returned to the pit of her stomach.

They weren't that close to the highway. She kept that fear to herself as wrapped her arms around Keegan's waist, bearing down behind his back to avoid the chilly wind.

It was less than thirty minutes later that Keegan followed the front ATV to a slow stop. The two officers in front dismounted their four-wheeler and strode back to Keegan.

"We can go right of the Apache Basin or left of it, but we can't go through it. We'd get stuck. And, once we pass, if we don't see anything, then we need to head back to base and tag team another group in. I'm low on fuel."

Bo's heart sank. They couldn't give up. They couldn't!

But they had to. Defeated but with the shadow of a hope clinging to her heart, she sat quietly as the men agreed to bear right and head back to camp in order to avoid a separate rescue mission.

"Don't worry, Bo," Keegan called over his shoulder. "They're out here somewhere. It's a big forest, but they're here."

Forever later, they'd arrived back at base camp to learn that a secondary search had broken off in the direction of the basin and choppers were honing in on the point of the crash. Before they had left the plane, Keegan propped a flood light on its nose, directing crews to scope the area.

It was just a matter of time, Keegan assured her and her parents as they reconvened for a brief drink before Bo insisted on going back out. She wanted to see the other side of the basin. That had to be their location.

Stifling a yawn, Keegan checked his watch but agreed easily, requesting a brief restroom break, first. Bo did the same after bringing Anna up to speed. She had been shivering near a campfire, fretting over nubby fingernails and a half-eaten bagel. Dutch, who either couldn't handle Anna's weeping or genuinely cared about the quest (Bo suspected the latter, actually) asked to go with this time.

But before they left, the Air Force contact crackled into Keegan's radio. Frowning, he stepped up toward the road and away from Bo and Dutch and the others. Bo studied him as he leaned his head far down onto his chest and crossed his free arm under the other, pacing back and forth, a few steps left, then a few steps right, never once looking up to meet her eyes.

She glanced up at Dutch, who was looking at Anna who was covering her mouth with her hands before she found Bo's gaze. She pulled them down and asked, her voice low, "What do you think happened?"

"Maybe they're just touching base about the wreckage site," Bo offered, her headache returning with a vengeance.

Bo looked to Dutch for input, but he simply crossed his arms and kept his focus on Keegan. After what felt like an hour but was probably less than five minutes, Keegan shook his head briskly and clicked off, stowing his radio before rejoining them below.

"Okay, chopper found the plane and they are doing what they can forensically. Some of the investigation is stalling because of the dark. We've lost volunteers, of course, and the Air Force is pulling some resources over to New Mexico, where another incident occurred about an hour ago."

Bo's face fell. "No way, we can't just end the search *now*," she stomped her foot, fully aware of the childish effect. Keegan ignored it and went on.

"We're not, but there is some good news. Here, let's walk over to your folks so they hear it, too."

The foursome kicked their way over to the campfire where Margaret was resting, Dick rubbing her shoulders above her. In any other circumstances, it would have looked sweet. Now, it just looked pathetic.

"Ma'am? Sir? We have an update," Keegan's manners got in the way of efficiency. *Just spill it, come on*, Bo tried to urge him by narrowing her eyes and nodding her head. *We're ready!* "A group of teenagers was in the woods earlier today. They mentioned it to their folks who called it in. Anyway, their location was damn near, excuse my language, was close to the wreckage site. Just east of the Basin."

"Did they see anything?" Margaret's eyes lit up, and she steadied herself against Dick before pushing off to be closer to Keegan and his good news. Bo brought her hands to her face, bracing for a big reveal. But Keegan wasn't the sort to heighten the excitement by downplaying the news.

"No," he confirmed. "They were out there some hours, they took one of their dad's UTVs and made it pretty deep into the forest before getting out and walking deeper. They said they heard about the disappearance and thought they'd go look. But, they didn't see anything. Or hear anything. However, the good news is we can focus our search on the area to the west of the Basin."

Anna and Dutch and Margaret and Dick all nodded in solemn agreement, but it didn't sit well with Bo. "Keegan, they aren't pulling the search from the south and east, are they? I mean teenagers aren't reliable." Her voice rattled with anxiety.

"No, no. Of course not. But we are going to reallocate some of the crews onto the west side. It's nearing day three, which is critical for exposure and hydration. It makes sense to hedge our bets. Don't worry, we'll keep a couple of crews on the entire perimeter."

Bo stabbed her parents with a look, prompting them to step up and say something. It was no good to reduce resources on the perimeter. Just because kids didn't hear anything east of the basin, well that meant nothing!

"Keegan," she began. He wiped a hand over his face and offered a small smile.

"Let's go, Bo. We'll take Dutch and head back out, east of the basin. Okay?"

And with that, they took off. Of course, the whole bumpy, chilly ride, Bo prayed that radio static would interrupt their mission and let them know that Erica and Ben were found. *Alive. They were fine. Come back, now. Give your sister a hug.*

But an hour into the ride, still nothing.

Chapter 41: Erica

Her eyes fluttered open and shut to Ben's voice. Distant. Darkness absorbed the room, muffling his words. She had no sense of how long it had been since he'd deposited her on the sofa. Had she fallen asleep? Had she passed out? For a sagging, rotting, threadbare love seat, it was the most comfortable napping place she'd ever enjoyed. As far as she was concerned, she could stay here until rescue came.

She murmured as much.

"What?" Ben's voice answered, closer now. She pinched her brows together and peeked out one lazy eyelid. She'd have startled if she had more energy. His face was pressed against her forehead, but she hadn't even felt it at first. "What are you trying to say, Erica?" he asked.

She answered him. *Stay here.*

"I can't understand you, you're mumbling, Erica. Listen, it'll be dawn soon. We're leaving, okay? I'm going to take care of you Erica, you just have to stay awake. You can't fall asleep again. Neither of us can," he hissed into her ear, but she was so tired. Her eyes so heavy. Her leg hurt so much that nausea began to wave through her gut. At least it would keep her awake for him.

But she couldn't move. She had to stay there. She couldn't move.

"No." It came out as a groan. Her mouth filled with a gag and her head lolled to the side as a dry heave escaped from the back of her cottony tongue.

"Shhh, Erica, yes, we're leaving. I'll carry you."

"No, Ben," she was awake now. Another heave interrupting her attempt to convince him. "I'm staying. Go home. Take care of the boys. Come get me later," she whispered, her voice calm. She couldn't imagine worse misery, but she knew a rocky ride on Ben's shoulders would be just that. She'd die. For sure.

She was dying now.

She felt one arm snake beneath her neck and the other under her thighs.

Another heave. The pain.

"Ben, *stop*, *please*," she begged, crying now, dry sobs which caused her to gag again.

He said nothing but heaved her up in his arms.

"No, *Ben*," her voice was fading and she had little opportunity left. But she felt it inside her. She couldn't go. With every ounce of energy she had left she swung a hand at his face, slapping the rough skin and sobbing again at him. "Leave me, please, *Ben*."

"Dammit, Erica, you aren't dying here. I'm taking you home *now*. Just be quiet and hold still, *dammit*, Erica." She felt him bury his head in her neck as he pushed them out the door and into weakening darkness of the brisk, dewy morning. It was probably beautiful. A series of memories flashed through Erica's head, like a dream. Mornings on the farm. Collecting eggs at daybreak. Complaining about the cold to her mother as the woman wiped damp hands on an apron. The morning she went into labor with the boys. Ben holding her hand and rubbing her back as she heaved through contractions. The surgery room where both boys were ripped untimely from her womb. Mornings after. Feedings. Baby swings. Tummy time. Mornings years later on green baseball diamonds as the twins knocked home runs and dashed around the bases to Erica and Ben's cheers. The morning she took her last pregnancy test.

Positive.

The morning she began to bleed.

She dropped her hands to her sagging lap, her mouth falling agape in agony. "*Tell the boys I love them*," she whispered before closing her eyes for what was most certainly the last time.

Chapter 42: Ben

Ben knew it was bad. They were on day three of no water. No food. Day two of Erica's infection. She was fading fast. He had no time left. He should have started the night before, but he was so weak.

Now, he was even weaker.

But it didn't matter. He lifted Erica's waifish body off the couch, ignoring her faint protests and gagging. He couldn't carry her on his back. She seemed too fragile.

With her body draped across his arms, he ran. As fast he possibly could. Through trees and over roots, taking care to avoid what could be a fatal fall. He channeled his strength and the last of his energy but hearing her last request had almost made him want to give up with her.

Instead, he kept the boys in his mind's eye. He had to return with their mother. And soon.

Twigs and branches cracked beneath his shoes as he pushed and pulled breaths out and in. It focused him. He recalled his time playing football. Training days. Summer boot camps. Conditioning.

The sun finally began to bleed over the horizon and through the trees, its early warmth filling him with hope as the forest floor became clearer now. He ran faster, despite his exhaustion. The trunks became a blur and he tuned out Erica's moans, listening only for her breath and nothing more. As long as she was breathing she would make it. He could save her. He had to.

Running at near-full speed, moments flashed through his mind like missiles. The first time he had ever seen Erica. Her white-blonde braids mesmerized him from the story time circle in first grade. When he finally, by freshman year, worked up the courage to ask her on a date only to be told he'd have to ask their dad first. When she moved with him without question across the country. Their wedding day.

The day they had the twins.

The day she had her miscarriage.

Every day in between was like a nail on a coffin of doom.

And then, she'd finally asked.

But there, in the forest, they made up. He loved her. She loved him. They recommitted. How could he keep his new promise to her if she died?

A lump grew in his throat and tears threatened to spill from his eyes onto the thirsty skin of his face. He swallowed it down, glancing at the angel in his arms. Her eyes squeezed shut in pain. Thank God. She was still alive. Still feeling. That had to be good.

He beat down the grown-over path of the trailer, wondering just how far someone was willing to drive from the highway to a dinky property like that.

And then, as the path grew even denser, he heard it. A distant hum. He pulled to a stop and threw his head back, searching the sky until he saw it- a helicopter. Off to his right by hundreds of yards, probably. Did he stop, put Erica down, and wave? Or did he trust that this path would end soon?

He eyed the chopper, watching it drift, nose angled down, above. It was probably hovering over the basin. Rescue. At least people were looking for them, and they were dang close. He dropped his head, heaving deep breaths under the weight of Erica, whose eyes were now closed. He jostled her body. "Baby, wake up! Look! *Look!* A helicopter! We're going to be saved!"

All she offered as a reaction was to more deeply furrow her brow in pain. It was good enough for him. But as he lifted his head again to the chopper, it was farther away. *There's the answer.*

He hitched Erica tighter against his bare torso and took back off. At least he had a path. All he had to do was make it to the highway. No guessing game about direction. Just forward fast. He could do that. For his wife, he could do anything.

He'd expected the brush from the path to clear at some point. But it hadn't. And nor were there old campsites peppering the area, as he'd also expected. Or more litter. Or more signs of humanity. The trailer must have been older than he'd realized. Part of a forgotten region. The owner likely hoping something would come of the weedy land. It never did. And he had given up, abandoning the trailer with its roach motel and needles and dried marshmallows. Just gave up.

He swallowed the memory of his own feelings about his marriage. His own personal promise- the one he made weeks ago when he ordered the necklace. He told himself that if Erica hadn't appreciated it. Hadn't moved on for once and for all, that he would have asked *her* for a divorce. That she was thinking the same thing crushed him. That he was willing to give up over his own selfishness... deplorable. He'd made a vow, and he was going to change. Make everything work no matter what it took. He was going to change his life. Her life, too. And boys', too.

He tried to still his raspy breathing so that he could hear in case another chopper whizzed above. His focus trained ahead, he prayed to God that the path would clear, and a slice of highway would appear. Soon. Very soon. If it was possible, Erica's body was even heavier. But that didn't bother him. Her shallow breaths and bluish lips did. Her legs slapping up and down, loosening the tourniquet as he ran. That was the problem. He sped down the narrow, weedy lane, his thighs and calves cramping, his back slick with sweat, despite the cool morning air. Erica slipped up and down his damp chest, her hot skin scorching through her t-shirts. He wheezed, his lower back screaming in pain.

And then, a purring sound. Far away.

He dug his heels into the dry earth, adjusting Erica briefly before stilling himself, breathing sharply through his nose as he listened again. He spun in a circle, his head back as he searched the sky.

No helicopter, but a hum prevailed, consistent but unseen. He dropped his head and peered into the trees, looking for a flash of color, a spray of dirt underneath a jeep or motorcycle.

The hum grew louder and turned into the roar of an engine. He was certain of it.

"*HELP!*" He shouted over his wife's body. "*WE'RE OVER HERE!*" He paused, expecting the sound to crush his soul and move away, disappear among the trees.

But it didn't. He could now hear tires crunching over earth. He whipped around in circles as he called out for help, his voice scratchy and weakening by the syllable.

And then, there it was. A four-wheeler, speeding over brambles and between tightly rooted trees... toward Erica and him.

Could they see him?

He shouted once more, refusing to let his wife drop in order to wave his arms.

They saw him.

His vision narrowed on the driver, a tall man in a button-down. And, behind him, black hair whipping in the wind. A pale face peeking around. A thin arm waving wildly. Faint shouts returned his own, like an echo of hope.

It was Bo. And she was sitting behind a vaguely familiar face.

He glanced down at Erica, whose veins were glowing through the skin on her face. He looked to her thigh, now exposed after having lost the t-shirt yards ago. The cut was oozing white fluid. His heart raced as the ATV pulled up, and he finally caught sight of the second one behind. Two men he'd never met.

"Is she alive!?" screamed Bo as she hurdled off the vehicle and toward him, her eyes looking from his face to Erica's body.

"*Yes*." It came out as a breath rather than a word. And suddenly, he felt all of his own aches, but especially the thirst. "*Water*?" He cleared his throat, enunciating the simple word a second time.

The tall man rushed up behind, a plastic bottle gripped in his fingers. With no introduction, he cradled Erica's head in his hand, about to give her a drink, but Ben grabbed the bottle, doing it himself. Her eyes never opened, but she lapped at the water, her lips almost immediately regaining some color beneath the chapped skin. Bo held her head down to Erica, whispering into her sister's ear as she eyed Ben gratefully.

"*She got an infection*," his hoarse voice stumbled over the last word. "*Fever*."

"Here, I'll take her on my ride. She can fit between Bo and me. You join the others," the now-familiar-looking officer demanded.

Ben drew a sip from the bottle. The cool liquid doing wonders on his throat. After coming up for air, he shook his head. Taking a breath in through his nose, he answered. "No. I'll take her."

He pushed passed Bo and the familiar stranger and jogged to the ATV. He wrapped Erica's legs around his torso, pressing a hand to her skeletal back as he straddled the seat and waved Bo over.

She jumped on the back, and away they sped, taking the path. He thought he heard the second ATV rev behind him and join in the race, but he didn't care. He had to get her to the hospital. And he'd do it himself. As the path began to clear, he put the vehicle to the test, opening her up to reveal she could practically fly. He glanced at the gas tank. Half full.

"Ben!" Bo screamed into his ear. "Your dad is okay! He made it! He's alive!"

A tear fell from her Ben's eye as his face lifted into a smile. Maybe everything would be okay, after all.

Just minutes later, the path spat them out onto a familiar easement off of Maplewood Highway. He knew exactly where they were. Twenty minutes from the hospital in a car on a normal day. Ten if he sped.

He felt Erica move her head on his shoulder, saying something now to Bo, whose arms clung around Ben and Erica, gluing them together and holding her sister in place. As he peeled down the single lane, he glanced beneath his arm to see Erica's leg was lifted up. Bo must have been holding it.

The trio barreled down the highway, pulling up to the ER bay, where a throng of EMTs and doctors awaited them. Someone must have figured Ben's plan and radioed in.

The rest was a blur. Family had arrived immediately, scurrying around uselessly as police tried to contain them and the growing mass of rubberneckers. Once inside the lobby, and away from the rush of media and local folks, doctors and nurses lifted Erica onto a gurney, waving Ben off to a second one. He ignored them and instead ran alongside the wheeled bed with the others, gripping Erica's clammy, grubby hand in his own all the way until a security officer had to grab his arms and rough him back.

A nurse tried to prod him over to his own room, persuading him to lie down for an examination. But he refused, and instead posted up outside the double-doors behind which Erica was shivering and moaning and writhing in pain.

"I'm staying right here," he answered the pleading nurses, his arms crossed over his naked chest, his forehead caked in three-day-old blood, his eyes trained on the cloudy window through which all he could see was a second set of doors.

Feeling wholly rejuvenated after chugging a pitcher of water the nurse had brought to him, he now slumped down into the plastic chair she'd left there.

Sighing deeply, he let his head fall into his hands.

His dad was okay. Thank God.

Bo had also mentioned that the boys were safe at the lodge with Mary, which was another relief. He'd get to see them soon. But not too soon. He couldn't face them without Erica.

With no clock and no view of anything, Ben again felt like he had no sense of time. Had it been five minutes? Five hours? He gingerly touched a hand to his head, feeling the cut above his eyebrow, bearing through its dull throbs.

Then, the doors popped open beside him. Out strode a man in blue scrubs, his puffy hat crumpled in his hand.

"Mr. Stevens?"

Ben stood, offering his filthy hand to the doctor who graciously shook it. "How's Erica? Is she..." he swallowed, "Is she going to make it?"

The man nodded gravely. "Well, Ben," he began. Ben's eyes flashed behind them through the doors. Could she have... no. There was no way she'd died. She was talking on the ATV. She was holding his hand.

Tears formed in the corner of his eyes, he began to move to the doors. "Let me see her, please! One last time, at least. Please let me see her!" He was hysterical as he wiped at his face and began to push past the man and a nurse who'd overheard his commotion and stopped to help. The two put their hands up, holding Ben in place.

"Ben, she's okay. She's going to make it. But, her leg..."

A calmness washed over Ben as he heard the words. She was okay. She was going to make it. "Thank God, oh, thank you, Doctor," he answered before the white-haired man held up a hand another time.

"But Ben, her leg. The loss of blood coupled with exposure, it is in bad shape. I'm not the surgeon. I'm a nurse. Surgery has begun. I came out here because we wanted to bring you up to date. She's going to live. You did a great job, Ben. However," he paused as Ben searched his eyes, confused. "Ben, we aren't sure we can save her leg."

Ben's reaction was immediate and unwavering.

He didn't care. He didn't care if she was paralyzed or legless or anything else, as long as she was alive.

He shook his head at the two nurses. Fresh tears fell from his eyes and onto his lips as they formed a smile.

She was going to live.

One leg or no legs—whatever. He didn't care. As long as he could have his wife back.

Ben let the nurses leave him there, to sit back down in the plastic chair. He picked up his empty tumbler, trying for one more sip, though it was dry.

As he licked his lips, he thought back over the past three days. The past three weeks. Months. Years.

Ben realized he never should have cared about chasing a perfect life. A perfect city. A perfect job. All that had gotten him was a dying marriage.

Now that he had confirmation that Erica would make it, he knew without the shadow of a doubt that all along he had been chasing the wrong thing. A perfect job wasn't going to solve any of their problems. Perfect cars. A perfect house. No. Those things were the *problems* in their marriage. A grin pulled at the corners of his eyes as he pictured poor, desperate Bo. The elusive Harrison Vogel. His unkempt plane. The dead hawk. His father's health. All those pieces had, somehow, almost tragically, become their solution.

And hours later, when Ben was finally escorted in to see his beautiful, kind, smart, tough wife, Ben realized that being imperfect with Erica made everything perfect after all.

Epilogue

After surgery, Erica and Ben stayed in the hospital for a couple days. Ben's father visited them, which was nearly as emotional as the moment Ben learned Erica would live through the surgery.

When Bo brought the twins to the hospital for their first visit, Ben declared that he had an announcement. Erica and the boys listened in wonderment as he decided he would give up his position with Southwestern. Erica, for her part, protested, arguing that Ben should do what he loved. His response was simple: his family was his first love. He couldn't balance being a college coach and prioritizing the three most important people in his life. He picked them.

He agreed to finish the season with the team, and they would move again the following summer—out of the Tucson heat. But not back to Philly.

After leaving the hospital and returning to Tucson, Mary and Anna had called with an idea. They knew football season was well underway, but why didn't Erica and Ben spend their upcoming anniversary weekend at Wood Smoke? August in the mountains was lovely—they'd enjoy the getaway and have a chance to… reconnect in nature without the threat of black bears or rusty rebar. The two happily agreed and made plans for a quiet retreat.

Once the couple had found themselves back in their hometown, a new love was formed. Ben and Erica did reconnect, in more ways than one. That weekend, Erica made the family's next big decision:

They would return to Maplewood.

Ben's excitement was expected since he'd long missed the mountain, but when they told the twins, the double cheers caught Erica off guard.

"We get to live in the woods?" Luke replied, beaming out from his blonde mop.

"Near our cousins?" Nicky joined in.

"With our family, yes," Ben replied, reaching an arm around Erica's waist and pulling her in for a kiss.

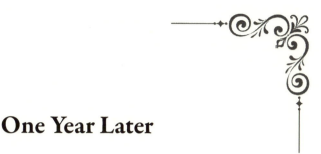

One Year Later

"Breathe, Erica," Ben whispered through the blonde wisps that tickled her ear. "Just breathe, baby."

"Sir, you're going to need to step aside," came the voice of an attending nurse. Ben glanced up at her, ready to argue, but she went on. "Just move over to the other side of the bed, please. I have to work this here machine." She gestured to a tangle of cords, not unlike the ones that had kept Papaw Stevens alive and a year before.

Ben dashed around the bed and behind her doctor, who was positioned squarely between Erica's two legs.

The scrubbed-up man barked orders up at her as Ben rejoined his wife, softening the man's words with his own translation. "Breathe, then push, you can do this." He peeked down toward the doctor's hands, past the slight scar on her thigh. He was desperately curious about the gender. Erica had refused to find out, declaring that she didn't care. Boy or girl, she was elated to add to their family. Anyway, she was too busy to care, what with taking her online coursework for a teaching certificate.

Her indifference probably encouraged Ben's curiosity. After all, if he was having a little girl, he needed to start preparing mentally, especially since he was Maplewood High's new head football coach. He'd be living the nightmare of teenaged locker room talk, and teaching those boys some manners would have to be a priority, especially if a little Girl Stevens would cheerlead there in fourteen years. Heck, maybe she'd even be on the team. With a mom as tough as Erica, anything was possible.

Ben repositioned his hand behind Erica's neck, massaging it until she cried out again in pain. It was a miracle that Erica was able to have a natural birth after her previous C-section. But she had advocated for it herself, insisting that she was strong enough. Really, she was.

Minutes later, Erica gave one heaving final push, and out popped a tiny pink towhead, wailing at the top of her little lungs.

Sometime later, as Ben and Erica were staring at the sleeping princess, a nurse came in to ask for the child's name for the birth certificate.

Ben and Erica answered at the same time, their words floating through the room in perfect harmony.

Roberta MaryAnn.

She was named for three women. The one who saved her parents' marriage. And the two who booked their anniversary weekend at Wood Smoke Lodge, where little Roberta was made just nine months earlier.

The End

Other Titles by Elizabeth Bromke

Christmas on Maplewood Mountain
Maplewood in Love
Return to Maplewood

A Note from the Author

Thank you for reading an independently published novel. When readers choose indie stories, they are single-handedly making a difference in the life of a passionate writer, because every copy *counts*. I hope you enjoyed *Missing in Maplewood*. If you have the opportunity, I'd be honored if you would write a review on Amazon or Goodreads.

Yours in reading,

E.B.

Acknowledgments

This book would be a shell of a story without the generous advisement of a few crucial people. I'd like to thank Robert Raterink with the Pima County Sheriff's Search and Rescue team for his insight on foot and air searches pertaining to missing persons and missing aircraft. Also, thank you to Allison Zettwoch, a private pilot and romance novelist who guided me through the experience of small plane turbulence and bird hits. Nancy Manhardt, my old friend and fellow Oro Valley native- thank you for helping narrate the experience of flying from Tucson to Show Low and your special knowledge of flight plan procedures as they pertain to the geography of the novel.

I'd also like to express my deep gratitude to Mr. Alton "Tom" Kingsbury, aviation and flight instructor, airplane inspector, and a man who has become a close confidant in my creative endeavors herein. Without Tom, there would be no Harrison Vogel and no Piper Cherokee, among many other crucial plot details. Thank you so much, Tom. I hope the story of Ben and Erica has landed with accuracy and style.

A big thanks to my early readers: Connie Chastain, author of southern romance and suspense novels, for your appreciation for Bo and my character development; Jackie Lee, author of *disORIENTED* and winner of Food Network's CHOPPED, for your spectacular advice on Erica; and Joseph Donne, author and friend, for your exhaustive work with my style, mechanics, and content. Jeff Robinson, as always—thank you!

I'd like to acknowledge my cover designer's terrific work on every book in this series. Thank you, GermanCreative for pulling together a beautifully branded and genre-appropriate piece of art using the photography of photoweges, sanneberg, and Andrew Lozovyi.

Last and never least, thank you to our family (Engelhards and Fiorillos/Bromkes)—our moms and aunts (and Kara!) for reading and supporting my efforts. Ed, you're amazing. Thank you for encouraging me and loving me. You are always the inspiration for the good parts of my heroes. And, Eddie. Always for you!

An Excerpt from Maplewood in Love

By Elizabeth Bromke

Chapter 1

Lips tingling, body numb. Mary felt immobile after that kiss. It told her everything and nothing. Attraction. Chemistry. Momentum. They had it all. But, it had only been two days. Two days of flirting in the snow. Two days of cuddling deep into the leather sofa as a fire blazed beside them. And in them.

Two days which resulted in a promise that they had only just begun. She sighed, smiling back at him as he pinned her with a gaze that only a tender-hearted man knew how to give. After tonight, when would they see each other again? To her, it wouldn't be soon enough. But she held firm that he would go to his bedroom, and she would go to hers. They'd have breakfast with the other guests the next morning. And then, of course, they set a plan that he'd return the next weekend. She went to bed holding that plan close to her heart because Mary Delaney was officially head over heels for one of her guests.

She jolted from her sleep, her sheets tangled about her, tendrils of hair tickling her face. Had the whole thing been a dream? A cruel Christmas present? Because it made no sense...

A fully booked Wood Smoke Lodge.

The CEO and founder of FantasyCoin.

And simple, little Mary Delaney, innkeeper for corporate retreats in the mountains of Arizona.

Yes. It was a dream.

A dream come true.

Filled with a hope she had seldom known, Mary rolled herself out of bed and into her little bathroom, where she inspected her face and hair. Fresh. Happy. Glowing, even. Her mind immediately recalled Kurt Cutler's handsome face, athletic build, and the clear green gaze of his stare. Never before could the wild-haired beauty fathom a life in which she would be kissing the president of a billion-dollar tech company.

Who just so happened to be her sister's boss.

The complications did not escape Mary Delaney.

Sighing lightly and offering her reflection a small, mischievous smile, she skipped makeup altogether and instead splashed cool water over her face before collecting her hair up on top of her head in a messy pile. Then, she pranced back out to her bed, digging beneath the rumpled duvet for her phone.

One text from her sister, Anna.

Sorry about everything, I guess. I'm home. Have a good week. Talk later.

Mary frowned. Although Anna's sour response was an example of her typical attitude, there was a certain tone to it that caught Mary off-guard. Had she gone too far in her own message the night before? She hadn't meant to. But after the magical evening with Kurt, she had just been feeling... honest. All she did was bring to Anna's attention her bad behavior from the days before. Anna's obvious jealousy was unappealing and disappointing.

Rest up. Recharge. Take care of yourself. You almost ruined the retreat for all of us, Mary had texted.

She didn't care if she was younger, she was right. Anna was in the wrong.

Now, as Mary flashed her eyes along her own words, their sharpness crystallized. She tapped out an apology.

Anna Banana. Sorry if I was harsh. I just care about you & want you to be happy. I'll call you when I get a chance. Love you lots. Hugs. <3

There. Mary felt better. She knew Anna was tough. She could take the truth, and she needed to hear it. Acting out in front of the FantasyCoin team was unbecoming. Anna needed to make some changes in her life. And, now that Anna had helped Mary through a hard spell by bringing business to the Lodge, Mary knew it was time to return the favor. Soon. Not now. Now, she had other important business.

She pressed the power button on her phone and tossed it back into the folds of her bedding before slipping out of her jammies and into worn jeans and a flannel pullover. She stuffed her feet into her fur-lined slippers and breezed out of the room, down the staircase and toward the kitchen, ready as ever to whip up her best breakfast for Wood Smoke Lodge's most handsome guest... and the other guests, too.

As she cornered the banister, it hit her: a wall of aromatic bacon, the drip-drip-drip of the coffee maker, the sizzle-and-flip-flap of pancakes on a griddle.

Mary cocked her eyebrow. Had Anna driven back and surprised her? Maybe she never left Maplewood... Was it Maci, FantasyCoin's social media manager, who had done little more than smudge her phone screen the whole weekend?

With hesitation, she shuffled in her slide-on slippers past reception and the great room sofas, running her hand along the back of the loveseat where she and Kurt had snuggled the night before. As she approached the open entryway to the kitchen, she saw him. The back of him, at least.

In a gray tee-shirt and flannel pajama bottoms stood Kurt Cutler, his arms working in tandem to maneuver sizzling strips of bacon from a cookie sheet onto a pile of paper towels precariously perched to the left of the stove.

Mary stopped, allowing a grin to spread across her face as she propped her hands on her slight hips. *Well, I'll be*, she thought. *A man who cooks.* As if he sensed her standing there in the doorframe, he whipped around, tongs in hand.

"Good morning, Mary." His voice took on a velvety effect, and she saw that he was wearing her pink, 'I'm a Bear in the Morning' apron. The scene was too much to handle, and Mary erupted into a fit of giggles.

Kurt smiled back before setting the tongs atop the row of bacon and striding to the petite brunette. He wiped his broad hands across the apron before wrapping them around her waist and pulling her up to him, nuzzling her neck and murmuring something about how good she smelled.

"I could say the same for you," Mary replied as she slid back down onto her heels and gently pressed away from his burly grip. "You can cook?" her eyes wandered beyond him to a crisping pancake on the griddle.

"Oh dang it," he muttered and dashed back to the stove, searching frantically for the spatula before slip-sliding the overcooked cake onto a growing pile of otherwise golden ones. "Whew," he breathed out and returned his eyes to her. "Not really. This is my first time with pancakes, I think." He haplessly gestured behind him and Mary could tell that he was praying she'd take over.

Effortlessly, she grabbed the sagging stick of butter from the edge of the counter and sliced it up, dropping little squares onto the griddle before scooping out three perfect circles of batter onto each square.

She plucked a piece of grease-slick bacon from the paper towels and bit off the end, crunching her way through the salty goodness before nodding up at her dark-haired guest. "Delicious. I'd say you're doing just fine without me."

Kurt returned her smile with his own. Mary could feel his gaze on her lips, but she wasn't about to kiss him right then and there. What if the other guests appeared? He seemed to quietly accept her decision, and they made light small talk as they finished preparing the breakfast together.

Soon enough, the other FantasyCoin team members dragged themselves downstairs in different stages of dress- some clearly packed and ready to head back home, down to Phoenix, and some still in their pajamas and bedhead hair-dos.

Running the lodge for the past ten years, Mary was used to this little morning parade. Even with the meager business she had been getting, it was always the same. The after-dawn hours brought out a certain truth about people. It was maybe her favorite part of the job to observe who of her guests were the types to get ready for breakfast and who were the types to barely make it for breakfast.

As everyone yawned themselves into position at the old farmhouse table in the dining room, Mary worked her magic at pouring coffee and doling out extra napkins and serving the food Kurt had cooked up.

She couldn't help but notice a bit of a stillness in the air as if the other guests had quickly caught on to Kurt and Mary's blooming love interest. No one had *seen* anything, but why else would he pitch in with breakfast? And why else did he duck out of the previous night's activities in favor of slipping away with her? Surely, they all knew.

And that was why it felt like a little punch to the gut when Kurt sat down to eat with his staff, leaving Mary to saunter off and take her breakfast in the kitchen, like the innkeeper she was. Of course, he definitely gave her a meaningful glance as she looked back over her shoulder, searching. And she could feel his eyes linger on her as she sashayed herself away from the slowly-waking-up pack of tech employees, but still...

Mary slowly stirred a spoonful of sugar into her coffee before starting in on the dishes. She hadn't taken two sips nor made it through washing up one serving plate before she felt the air behind her grow dense. She hesitated at the sink, a dish sponge sudsing in her wet hand. She listened through the spray of water as a pair of footsteps approached her from behind.

She should turn around. She should see if it was a company member who needed more syrup. But she knew it wasn't.

And his strong hands latching themselves onto her hips proved it. Mary felt her breath rush out from her lips as Kurt pinned her against the sink, reaching a long, muscled arm above her shoulder and shutting off the running water.

Chapter 2

Kurt was torn between carrying on in his role as FantasyCoin boss and succumbing to Mary's subtle seductions. Sure, he got it. Mary was not trying to overtly seduce him. She was even maybe trying to do everything in her power to NOT seduce him.

But it wasn't working. She was sweet and sexy and everything in between. *She was everything.* So, he sat down and made a brief show of digging into his own sloppy pancakes and overcooked bacon, but once Mary tucked herself away into the kitchen as if she didn't belong out there with him... he pushed away from the table and left his employers to chug coffee and bemoan the upcoming drive back down to to the valley.

As he strode into the kitchen, his eyes passed over Mary's slight frame and wild hair. He liked that she had thrown it up, allowing him a full view of her slender, porcelain neck, tendrils unfurling into the collar of her flannel top.

Whew. He could hardly control himself around her and had realized he was no longer afraid to show it. He quickly stepped up behind her and reached around her to shut off the water.

"I'll do that for you later. Let's take a walk." There was no question in his voice, but he braced himself for her protestation. She swiveled to face him, leaning back against the sink and pulling a dishcloth to dry her hands between them as if to give herself distance.

"Well, let me at least get these soaking, and anyway..." she looked up at him but he cut her off.

"I said I'll do them later. Okay?" He took her hands, lacing his long fingers through her dainty ones.

"Later? But you'll all be leaving soon. Isn't that right? 'On the road by ten.' That's what I heard some of your guys say?"

Kurt let a slow grin overtake his face.

"Well, Mary, I don't want to be presumptuous, but what do you think about me staying here another night? I could grab a shuttle back down the mountain tomorrow. It would give us a little… alone time," Kurt let himself breathe as he finally pitched it.

He had already done the research the night before when he couldn't sleep. Since he had let Mary's sister take his car back down the mountain in order to handle the server issues back at the main offices, he was stuck for a ride. He wouldn't dare think of Mary driving him home (although, down deep he'd hope she'd offer). So, he took to the weak internet signal that his phone emitted in his little guest room upstairs, where he searched for taxi companies, private drivers, even nearby airports. He hadn't found the former two, but he did alight on a local private airline in the next town over. No flights until spring, however. Something about the business changing hands. Finally, after digging through the classifieds on the town's online newspaper, he stumbled upon a podunk shuttle company that made daily trips down to Phoenix and back up to Maplewood.

He was certain Mary would be over the moon. They could fully explore the fact that they were obviously falling for each other. *He* could find out if this was it: if this was what he had been waiting for. Mary could find out how good of a man he really was. That maybe being from the big city gave him an edge on his mountain man counterparts.

Kurt carefully measured Mary's reaction, watching as the look of question in her eye hardened into… fear? It couldn't be.

"Stay the night? You mean…" she faltered, searching the space around him for what to say next. "You mean… here? At Wood Smoke?" She bit down on her lower lip, her eyebrows knitted together in worry.

What was he missing?

Kurt took half a step back, keeping her hands in his. He couldn't pinpoint the clamminess to either his or hers. He licked his lips.

"Oh, um. No, no, no. I didn't mean to impose or…" he let one of her hands go and scratched the back his head, nervously. "I meant, I thought…"

What could he say to salvage this? Sure, they had only barely kissed the night before. But, Mary practically professed her love. And he did, too. He assured her he wasn't out for some weekend one night stand, and he really wasn't.

That's why he wanted to stay. To see this through. See if they could maybe take this early infatuation and make it something more.

Mary's face cleared and a devilish look took hold of her delicate features. "Kurt Cutler, spit it out. Do you want to stay the night in Maplewood? Or do you want to stay the night *with me*?"

MARY WAS TAKEN ABACK at first. She had made it very clear the night before that she was no Anna. She valued tradition and depth and all the things that early intimacy would hardly promise her. She had only ever kissed Kurt and just two other men in her entire life. If he thought he was going to schmooze her into something more than that, he wasn't listening.

But she knew he was, in some weird way, earnest. Because taking a shuttle on a nearly four-hour drive back down the treacherous canyon and into Phoenix was a miserable experience, and it surely would be for someone who drove a sports car and likely had easy access to a private jet.

Mary was clever enough to see he was, in some way, trying. For what, she couldn't quite tell. She thought for a minute. He *could* stay at the lodge with her. She could take him on a tour of Maplewood later that day. It'd be fun. They would keep to their separate rooms come evening. It would be... *appropriate*.

"I just want to spend time with *you*, Mary," he murmured at last.

But something nagged at her.

"Kurt, I'm incredibly, unbelievably, terrifically attracted to you," she finally replied as she pulled herself back into him and rested one hand against his taut chest. She glanced down for a split second before committing to what she did next. "But," she locked eyes with him and moved her hand from his chest to the back of his neck. "Let's stick to the plan we made last night." And with that, she drew his head down to hers and pulled him into the longest kiss she had ever had in her life.

Once they parted, she peeked over his shoulder at the entrance to the dining room, ascertaining that the other guests weren't watching on at their voluptuous display of affection. Seeing the coast was clear, she then looked to Kurt's face. It had softened. His eyebrows set back in their perfectly symmetrical positions above his light, clear eyes. His tongue slid over his lower lip before his mouth pressed close in satisfaction.

"Christmas on Maplewood Mountain, right?" He smiled down at her and ran his thumb along her cheek.

"That's right. In fact, maybe you can even meet my family."

Chapter 3

He had to keep himself from choking on his own reply. *Her family*? Now it was *his* turn to hesitate at *her* idea.

"Um, well I would love to spend next weekend with you, of course," he stalled and gently released her hands, tucking his into the soft cotton pockets of his pajama pants. He began to kick at the wooden floor with his socked foot like a pouting teenager.

Out of the corner of his eye, Kurt saw Mary bring her arms across her chest and cock her weight onto one hip.

"So what is it that you *really* want, after all, Kurt Cutler?"

He looked up, meeting her gaze with his own and having nothing to say in response.

Kurt and his employees left soon after this little spat with Mary. If you could even call it that. But he did. It was like their first little fight as a burgeoning couple. Or, at least, he thought of them that way.

When Mary drew a line in the sand about plans for the following weekend, he had no idea how to reply. He had misjudged her somewhat. Gone was the bare-faced beauty who scurried from the dining room to sip her coffee meekly in the kitchen. Her coy smile and knowing glances dissolved.

Was she a... prude? He didn't think so. If there was a word Kurt would use to describe her it wouldn't be prude. She had values. She had standards. But underneath both of that, she had passion.

She wasn't a prude. She was a tease.

And yet, Mary's hardened expression thrilled him. He could play her game. He wanted her badly enough. But, even so, he had no response to the family meet-and-greet idea.

So, he and the rest of his company members left.

When he made it home to his sterile Downtown condo, he immediately regretted his hesitation with her. He had a chance and he blew it. So he did the only thing a reasonable man would think to do: nothing.

He didn't call her or text her. He didn't even bring it up to Anna in the office on Monday. It was as if the weekend never happened. And all because he wasn't immediately comfortable with meeting Mary's family over Christmas.

Still, Kurt was a man falling in love. So, finally, come Wednesday, he was ready to act. He arrived at the FantasyCoin offices a little crumpled from four nights with no sleep and nothing on the brain except his wild-maned hostess. As soon as he breezed in through the main office door, he beelined for Anna's desk.

"Hey, Anna," he started.

"Hi, Kurt." She didn't look up from her computer. Instead, she clicked away with particularly pointy pink fingernails.

"How's Mary?" He tried to act casual. "And you. How are you today?"

That stopped her. Her fingertips paused mid-keystroke, her lips parted, and she looked up at him from beneath her red hair.

"I'm fine. I haven't really talked to Mary. I figured you had?" For the first time since before the weekend retreat, he saw Anna break into a smile. An evil smile, but a smile nonetheless.

He had to cover for himself. "Yes, I... I have. I just...I was just curious," he fumbled. "Anway, I actually wanted to come over here and discuss some of the agenda items for tonight's board meeting," he lied. But, it worked. Her smile faded and she returned to her computer screen.

"Oh? What's up?"

He did a poor job of stumbling through something about marketing and customer service surveys before finally excusing himself to go to his own desk.

By the end of the workday, he felt like punching someone or something. As the rest of the office left for the evening, Kurt hung back. Once he was alone, he dug his phone from his pocket and pulled up Mary's number, silently thanking himself for getting it from Anna before the retreat. Before he changed his mind, he hit dial and held the black device up to his ear.

One ring. Two rings. Five rings and a voicemail greeting later, Kurt hung up.

But he didn't *give* up. He opened his messaging app and navigated to the first and only text convo he had had with Mary, from the week prior.

He scrolled back through their few messages, reminding himself of seeing her picture for the first time on Facebook and then following through with generic "how's the weather" texts.

He moved his finger along the smartphone, tapping out what felt like the most important message in his life.

Hi Mary. Sorry about leaving so quickly on Sunday. I'm really looking forward to visiting you this weekend.

He hesitated, barely, before adding,

And your family, too.

SHE HAD SPENT THE LAST couple days tidying up after the big retreat. Mary had no bookings until after Christmas and so decided she would wait to begin her marketing blitz until closer to the New Year when the snowboarders and skiers were sure to start planning their trips to the slopes.

There just wasn't enough to do to preoccupy her worried mind. Mary knew she shouldn't *worry* about Kurt, but that's what it felt like. Worry that he wasn't the man she thought he was. Worry that she had overstepped some invisible boundary by introducing the topic of meeting family despite the fact that he and she hadn't even been on a date, much less declared any sort of relationship status.

Then, her stubborn side took over, convincing herself that Kurt Cutler would have to just take her or leave her. Mary wasn't the sort to hide her devotion to her family or her commitment to the idea of a true courtship, as opposed to whatever it was her three sisters engaged in. Mary thought about exactly what that was. Her three older sisters had been her only real reference for what dating and romantic engagements looked like.

Hook-ups for Anna. Except, of course, Danny Flanagan. That one she would never forget.

Forbidden love interests for Bo. Like that time she dated her professor. Another catastrophe.

And, well, Erica had naturally gotten married right away, so she and her perfect husband and perfect children and perfect world weren't even a point of comparison.

Besides, Mary longed for yesteryear and its simplicity, which was exactly why she idealized the notion of an old-fashioned arrangement. One in which Kurt would earn her father's blessing then demand that things progress carefully in the direction of a firm commitment. With any luck, that commitment would be a proposal, a brief-but-blissful engagement, and then a snow-white wedding.

After years of a stagnant life, Mary was ready to take the bull by the horns. And if Kurt was put off by it, then he wasn't *the one*. It was never too soon to rule a man out.

So, when Mary got exactly what she wanted, she didn't play around.

That's the right answer. I'll call with details tonight ;)

And with the punch of a SEND icon, Mary got ready for the rest of her life.

Did you love *Missing in Maplewood, A Novel*? Then you should read *Maplewood in Love* by Elizabeth Bromke!

Can love at first sight... last?

Mary will be turning thirty soon, and with each passing year she roots herself more firmly in her old-fashioned ways and traditional notions of courtship. She is determined to get married and start a family... but only if she meets the perfect man: one who can wait for her.

Kurt Cutler is divorced and tired of life in the big city. Sure, he has his billion-dollar tech start-up and all the freedom that big money can offer. But, is money enough? Will his past keep Kurt from having the one thing he has always wanted?

Mary Delaney and Kurt Cutler only met two days ago, but happily-ever-after already feels close within their reach. Download *Maplewood in Love* to find out if they can move from first kiss to forever in this fast-paced short read.

Read more at https://www.elizabethbromke.com/.

About the Author

Elizabeth Bromke is the author of the Maplewood Sisters series, a five-book saga following the Delaney sisters and their ups and downs in life and love. Each title is a standalone read.

Elizabeth lives in a small mountain town in Arizona. There, she enjoys her own happily-ever-after with her husband and their young son.

Read more at https://www.elizabethbromke.com/.

Made in the USA
Middletown, DE
22 November 2020